LUCKY

LUCKY

Chris Hill

WITHDRAWN

Chicken House

SCHOLASTIC INC. / NEW YORK

Library of Congress Cataloging-in-Publication Data

Hill, Chris (Chris Ann), author.
Lucky / by Chris Hill.—First edition.
pages cm
Summary: Lucky is a young red squirrel who was rescued from a hawk and now must somehow make his home among the Cloudfoot clan of larger, gray squirrels who live in the city park—and trouble is brewing, for the rival gray squirrels known as the Northenders are planning an invasion.
Includes bibliographical references.
ISBN 978-0-545-83977-8
1. Eurasian red squirrel—Juvenile fiction. 2. Gray squirrel— Juvenile fiction. 3. Identity (Psychology)—Juvenile fiction. 4. Social acceptance—Juvenile fiction. 5. Friendship—Juvenile fiction. [1. Red squirrels—Fiction. 2. Gray squirrel—Fiction. 3. Squirrels—Fiction. 4. Animals—Fiction. 5. Identity—Fiction. 6. Self-confidence— Fiction. 7. Friendship—Fiction.] I. Title.

PZ7.1.H56Lu 2016
823.92—dc23
[Fic]

2015024728

10 9 8 7 6 5 4 3 2 1   16 17 18 19 20

Printed in the U.S.A.   23
First edition, March 2016
Book design by Mary Claire Cruz

To my family
. . . and other animals

The Albion Park

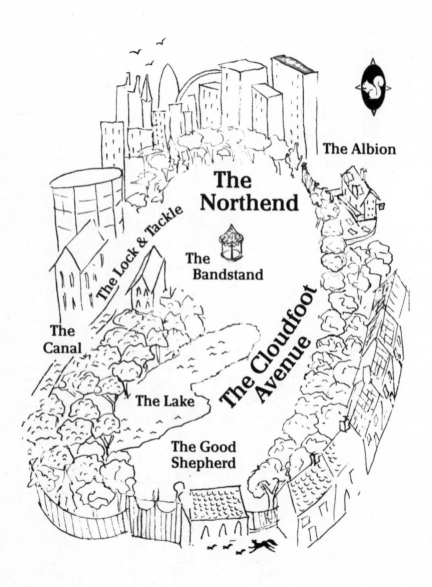

The Albion

The Northend

The Lock & Tackle

The Bandstand

The Canal

The Cloudfoot Avenue

The Lake

The Good Shepherd

1

Cloudfoot Avenue

Lucky?" It was a soft voice, a kindly voice, pulling him out of the Darkness. "Lucky squirrel, you're shaking again. Are you awake?"

Awake? I don't want to be awake, he thought. *It's happened again. This isn't my home-tree. I've woken up on Cloudfoot Avenue—again!*

"It's all right, Lucky, you're safe with me."

I'm not going to open my eyes yet. I'm going to breathe slowly and stop shaking. It's happening again today, but maybe tomorrow I'll wake up back home. But will I? Ever?

Lucky had lost count of how many times he'd thought this. Every day he hoped he'd be back in his home-tree again, snug and safe in his own drey-nest. Yet every day he woke up in an alien world with this creature who called herself a squirrel.

She said he was safe—she said she was his mother now. But she wasn't *right*. She didn't even look like a squirrel, with her horrible gray fur that smelled of smoke and dust.

He knew she wasn't right. He knew he'd had a mother before this "First Daughter" squirrel, brothers and sisters too. For a fleeting moment, just as he woke, he could remember them. Then they slipped away, replaced by memories of shrieking wind, splintering wood, and sharp talons.

Then, thankfully, the Darkness came again.

Maybe my family are just a dream, he thought. *But I know I'm not named Lucky, and I know you're not my mother!*

He never said it to First Daughter. She was kind to him and it would hurt her feelings.

"Lucky, I know you're awake!"

He opened his eyes obediently and looked up at the strange squirrel who wanted to be his mother. She smiled and nuzzled him out of the warm moss-lined bed at the base of her drey-nest. He uncurled and stretched. First Daughter towered over him. Even with nose and tail extended he was half her size. Why wasn't he getting any bigger?

Bud and branch, thought First Daughter, *am I doing the right thing? I can't keep him hidden in my home-tree forever, but he's so small!*

She'd tried to feed him up. Maybe he was supposed to be this small? Perhaps this was normal squirrel size in *his* home-trees. His fur was a peculiar red color, and his ears . . . She didn't even want to think about his ears . . .

There's nothing more I can do, she thought. *I must stop worrying.* So she began the morning grooming, cleaning his face and strange tufted ears with her sharp little tongue.

Lucky wriggled and started to giggle—it always tickled! First Daughter smiled again. He'd stopped shaking and seemed happier now.

A scratching noise outside the drey stopped her in mid-stroke. Lucky stiffened and wrinkled his nose. There were other creatures out there. He could smell them.

"Stay here, Lucky, I won't leave you for long."

First Daughter's drey was a hollow ball of tightly woven twigs, a warm and dry nest. She pushed through a small hole in the curved wall, arched over the edge, and jumped out onto her home-tree, where the drey hung safely between two great spars of wood.

I'm not going to hide in the moss-bed, thought Lucky. *I'm not going to be afraid.* So he crept up to the drey wall, straining to hear fragments of conversation over the rustle of leaves and unfamiliar distant rumbling sounds.

"It's too early for the Cadet Troop." This was First Daughter; he knew her voice.

"Tooth and claw, sister, why waste time?" This was not a friendly voice.

"The Ma gave him to me and he *is* growing . . . slowly."

"Sister, I have heard the chatter in the trees. I've heard that he's . . . different. A runt at best, and certainly not a Cloudfoot!"

"I will be the judge of that!" First Daughter sounded angry now. "He will join the Cadet Troop when he is ready, like any other Cloudfoot male."

"Then he will fail and be Cast Down. The Ma will not have weaklings in the Clan."

"I do not need *you* to tell me the Word of Ma, sister! He is my son and I will raise him."

Lucky could hear First Daughter coming back into the drey and he scurried down to the moss-bed. He thought she would look angry—she had *sounded* very angry—but she just looked sad.

"Different"? What did the other squirrel mean? It was First Daughter who was different, not him! They had been talking about him for sure, but what was this "Cadet Troop" he was supposed to join, and who was this "Ma"? She didn't sound very nice—or motherly! There were so many questions he wanted to ask, but First Daughter just carried on with his grooming as if nothing had happened. Eventually she considered him clean enough and seemed to come to a decision.

"Lucky, we are going out into the Avenue, into the Cloudfoot trees."

"Today? Now?" His whiskers quivered—going outside!

"It's time you learned about our Clan. I have kept you in my drey for too long. But you must promise to stay close and do everything I say. Understand?"

Lucky nodded solemnly. He was far too excited to be afraid. There was a world outside the drey-nest and somewhere, somewhere in that world, was his real home. *I'm going to find it*, he thought. *My family is out there somewhere!*

First Daughter squeezed through the gap in the woven twig wall. Lucky followed, small enough to slide through easily. He took a deep breath and dove over the edge of the drey, landing on a thick branch high up in a densely leafed tree.

His nostrils instinctively flared, tasting the air. Was this like his home-tree? He had a memory of its scent: clean pine, carried on sweet air. The air in this tree had a bitter, smoky tang. This did *not* smell like his home-tree.

First Daughter started to spiral up the thick tree trunk to the next branches. Lucky set off after her, circling the trunk, but she was really fast and soon disappeared among the huge green leaves. Lucky froze in panic, his claws pressed into the rough tree bark—he'd already lost her!

"Lucky!" First Daughter hung from the branch above him. "Come on, you must keep up!"

Lucky clawed up the rest of the trunk, trying to go as quickly as he could.

Bud and branch, thought First Daughter, *he's too slow. He's never going to survive at that pace!*

The two squirrels set off along the branches, leaping from tree to tree. This was better. Lucky was light and agile and he found thin branch pathways that First Daughter was too heavy to use. He was keeping up with her quite well now.

I've got to build up his stamina for climbing, she thought. *I'll have to. No slow squirrel survives for long.*

They were passing a large, beautifully woven drey in a chestnut tree when a female squirrel appeared. *She looks just like First Daughter*, thought Lucky. Waddling behind her, with a sour look on his face, was a young male.

Lucky was stunned. He'd expected to find *some* squirrels that looked like him, but all these Cloudfoots were strange. The young male didn't just have stubby small ears and dirty gray fur, he had a massive stomach too. This squirrel was bigger and fatter than any squirrel ought to be.

"Sister! Finally out with your *son*, I see."

Lucky recognized the voice and felt First Daughter stiffen. This had to be the other squirrel from outside the drey, the one who'd said he was different.

The other squirrel shoved the sullen male toward them. "Nimlet, say hello to First Daughter and her *son*."

Nimlet looked at Lucky and wrinkled up his nose in disgust. "You stink."

"You stink too!" said Lucky before he could stop himself.

The fat squirrel's mother tried not to laugh. "Nimlet!" she exclaimed. "The *poor* thing can't help how he smells—*or* what color he is."

First Daughter was furious. "Lucky, we are going *now*."

They traveled some way among the branches before First Daughter stopped.

"Sorry," said Lucky quickly, before she could tell him off. "But he started it!"

"I know. He has no manners and neither does my sister, Second Daughter. I'm sorry too, Lucky, but be careful what you say, otherwise you'll get into fights."

"I'm not afraid of getting into fights!"

Good, thought First Daughter, *but you're not big enough yet to win them.* "Fighting is no good without strategy, Lucky. In our trees the Cloudfoot Daughter Generals use their wits to win battles. It's called the Knowledge. They are the cleverest females in the Avenue."

"I can be clever too!"

First Daughter was taken aback. It had never occurred to her that a male might be clever. Males followed the Daughter Generals' orders and defended the Avenue—they didn't need to think for themselves. But Lucky wasn't big and strong like the Cloudfoot males, and it didn't look like he was ever going to be, so he would *need* to be able to think for himself—if he was to have any chance of survival.

I could teach him the Knowledge, she thought. *If he could plan for the future, understand strategy, and think logically, he'd have an advantage over the other males. It would be worth a try . . .* She looked down at his big bright eyes and trembling whiskers. "Would you like to learn to be *really* clever?" she asked.

"Oh, yes!"

"Come along then; we will start with some geography."

They spiraled higher up the tree trunk, leaving the densely foliaged, safe Mid-levels behind. Lucky tried to stay close, but it was hard work and the trunk seemed to go on forever. When they finally got close to the Canopy, the highest branches, he was panting and struggling for breath in the foul-smelling air. The branches had thinned out and leaf cover was scarce at the very top of the trees. The squirrels were exposed to the vast sweep of the sky.

"First rule: Check the airways," said First Daughter. "*Always* check the airways. The sky is dangerous—look!" She pointed to the black shapes circling above.

Lucky squinted upward as First Daughter listed the hunting birds that saw squirrel as a tasty snack. Thuggish crows and ravens. Thieving magpies, fast and clever. The silent swooping owls at dusk; they would happily pluck a squirrel from the trees if they could.

"Know the shape of your enemy, Lucky, so you can avoid them."

They went up higher, scanning carefully for incoming birds, and finally First Daughter led him out onto a viewing branch and showed him her world.

Lucky looked at it in horror: a long line of huge trees, stretching into the distance, as far as the eye could see. None of them had the shape or smell of any tree he knew.

"This is the Cloudfoot Avenue."

One side of the Avenue was bordered with strange shapes, square and pointy at the same time, that covered the whole of the landscape. Lucky had never seen anything so ugly.

"Houses," explained First Daughter. "Human dreys."

The other side of the Avenue was a vast flat sea of green, then more houses and towering white blocks on the horizon.

"That is Albion Park."

Lucky fought a rising tide of panic. *I'm trapped!* he thought. *Trapped between these "human dreys"!* He wanted to run. This wasn't a real wood or a forest—this wasn't a proper place for squirrels!

He frantically scanned the trees for any other squirrels like him. Any hint, any clue, anything he might recognize—any way back.

"I can't see my home-tree," he whispered.

"This is your home now," said First Daughter.

Lucky struggled hard to hold back his tears.

2

Mazie Trimble

Mazie Trimble scurried along the Mid-levels, leaping expertly from branch to branch, trying to look busy. This wasn't difficult; she was in the Foraging ranks and foragers were always busy collecting and storing food. But she didn't want any Senior Daughter stopping her with an errand to run—not today.

First Daughter wanted to see her!

At first Mazie had thought she might be in trouble again—she wasn't very good at taking orders from the stupid females who outranked her. But this didn't seem likely. First Daughter would be the next Ma one day; surely she wouldn't bother with a humble forager like Mazie?

It was a puzzle, and she was normally good at puzzles. She'd gotten the highest grade in her class for Strategy and Tactics. Everyone knew she was clever. Mazie knew she was clever.

But being clever wasn't enough for a female in the Cloudfoot Avenue. Mazie had discovered that you needed *connections*—the right breeding, or support from the powerful Daughter Generals—to be promoted in the ranks. There was no chance of that for a Trimble.

I should be a Daughter Attendant, she thought bitterly. *I'd be brilliant! But I'm stuck finding food.*

But now it seemed her luck might have changed. Her heart thumped against her chest as she entered First Daughter's drey. Could this be it? Had First Daughter recognized her talents? She bristled with excitement. *Please, please let this be the day!*

"Ma'am, you sent for me?" Mazie bobbed formally.

First Daughter could hardly disguise her shock. The last time she had seen Mazie Trimble was at the end of the Knowledge Trials. Then, she had been glowing, happy, and triumphant, with a Special Commendation for her achievement.

Now the young female's face was pinched and she was twitching nervously. It was a hard life in the Foraging ranks.

"Miss Trimble, my current Attendant will soon be promoted and there will be a space in the branches of my home-tree."

The young squirrel's face lit up—yes!

"Of course, that space would only go to a Daughter who was completely loyal and had won my trust, you understand?"

Mazie nodded frantically in agreement—of course she understood.

"Word of your skill in foraging has reached my ears," continued First Daughter, "and I wondered if you'd like to take on a pupil?"

"Oh, yes, ma'am!" exclaimed Mazie. "I am at your command."

"Do I have your word on that?"

"Absolutely," said Mazie firmly.

"Good," said First Daughter, "then I will introduce you to my adopted son."

Lucky stepped out from behind First Daughter's tail and did a little bob of greeting as she had taught him. It was hard to ignore the look of horror on Mazie's face, but Lucky had discovered that most Cloudfoots looked at him like that at first, and he was getting used to it.

Mazie's mouth opened and closed like a goldfish's. She had no idea what to say. She'd heard the chatter in the trees that First Daughter's baby was different, but nothing had prepared her for *this*. She would be the laughingstock of the Clan if she were seen with this . . . this *mutant*!

First Daughter had obviously read her mind. "Lucky

must not be seen learning to forage—so you will need to do this secretly."

"Of course, ma'am," said Mazie. That, at least, was a relief. "When shall I begin?"

"You will begin now, Miss Trimble. Lucky will be joining the Cadet Troop very soon and we have not a moment to lose."

The Cadet Troop? thought Mazie. *No chance! That male's crow bait for sure!* But she kept her thoughts to herself, and declared again that she was at First Daughter's service and would do her very best. Then she took Lucky to the most secluded part of the Avenue and began the task. After all, how hard could it be?

Lucky was keen to learn and First Daughter had told him that Mazie was clever and could teach him a lot. But being clever doesn't always make for a good teacher, as Mazie soon discovered. Everything she knew as a Cloudfoot-born-and-bred was new to Lucky. She would have to start from scratch.

"We'll begin with the trees." They were perched on the branches of a graceful silver birch overlooking the Park.

"Lesson one. This is a good tree," said Mazie.

"Why?"

"What d'you mean, *why*?"

"*Why* is it a good tree?"

"Because it *is*," said Mazie. "Everyone knows that."

"But I don't know! Is it because the trunk's a funny color?"

"No, stupid," she said crossly. "It's because it's the first to bud after the time of No-Growth."

"Why is that a good thing?"

Mazie was completely exasperated now. "It just is," she said crossly. He knew nothing! *Wait until he's shivering and starving in the bare branches through No-Growth*, she thought. *Then he'll understand.* Any tree that heralded the start of Bud-time was a good tree.

"So what's a bad tree then?" asked Lucky.

"The oak," said Mazie promptly, "because—"

"It's the last to bud?"

Mazie stopped and gave him a hard stare. Maybe he wasn't so stupid after all.

They moved down to the lower levels. "Those are good bushes," she said, pointing.

Lucky looked hard at the undergrowth below them—they all looked the same to him. "Why?"

"Because they have berries, of course!"

"But they haven't got any berries."

"Well, no, not yet, but they'll have berries soon."

"Well, how I am supposed to know then?" asked Lucky.

It was a fair question, but Mazie just twitched her tail in annoyance and scurried up the tree trunk. Lucky followed as quickly as he could, but she was very fast and he had to stop and catch his breath.

Out on the sea of green that was the Park, he could see lots of humans being taken for walks by their dogs. Some of the humans had two wheels instead of legs and glided over the ground. How strange! Fascinated, Lucky moved out along the overhanging branches to get a better view. A group of humans were running frantically along the path. *Something terrible must be chasing them*, he thought. He tiptoed out to the thin end of the branch, straining to see what sort of creature was hunting humans.

Mazie had gone a long way up the birch tree before she realized that Lucky wasn't following her. *Tooth and claw!* she thought. *Where has the useless male gone? I'll have no chance of promotion if I lose him.* She spiraled down the trunk calling his name. *Please, please don't be lost*, she thought as she darted backward and forward among the leaves. Finally she ran out onto an overhang to get a clearer view. Yes! There he was, below.

"Lucky, come back to the trunk!"

He waved up at her. "Why are the humans running?"

"I don't know!" yelled Mazie. She was furious. "Stop asking stupid questions and get back to the trunk *now*!"

"Why?"

"It's not safe out there, you dumb—" A shadow flickered over the sun and her fur instinctively rose. Oh, no! "Incoming!" she screamed, pointing to the sky.

Lucky looked up and froze. A huge black bird, all beak and snapping wing, was swooping down toward the tree.

"Get down!" she shrieked wildly. "Move! Move!"

The bird let out a *caw!* of delight as he spotted Lucky. This would be easy game—the squirrel wasn't even running! His sharp talons stretched out for the kill as Lucky threw himself off the branch in terror. The bird's claws closed around his tail—a second too late.

Lucky tumbled toward the ground with wind pounding in his ears, crashed through the bushes below, and lay stunned on the ground. The bird circled above, cawing in anger—where was the meat now?

Mazie leapt frantically down the tree. She couldn't see him—where was he? The sounds had alerted a group of young humans who were running toward the trees. The bird swooped again, but the human young were closing in. *Caw!* He rose back into the sky, disappointed. No squirrel for lunch today.

Mazie found Lucky under the bushes, limp and barely conscious. She crouched by his side as the human young circled the undergrowth, searching for the fallen squirrel. Lucky started to whimper.

Keep quiet! Please, please keep quiet, Mazie thought. Then the young humans were called away, and ran off laughing and screaming. Mazie let out a sigh of relief. "Get up!" She shook Lucky roughly.

He staggered to his feet groggily; he was trembling and badly bruised. There had been falling, and a bird—but no Darkness . . .

"Up the tree," ordered Mazie. "Now!" He followed her clumsily to the first branches, where she stopped and glared at him furiously. "Why are you called Lucky?" she demanded.

"Er . . . I don't know." He hadn't expected this question.

"Well, *I* do! Because for the most *stupid* male I've ever met, you're lucky to be alive!"

3

The Albion

Mazie stomped back to First Daughter's drey with Lucky trailing behind. *I've failed already,* he thought. Check for incoming—*I didn't even think—what will First Daughter say?*

Mazie bobbed a greeting and shoved Lucky in front of her. "All present and correct, ma'am," she said stiffly.

"Thank you, Miss Trimble—and what have you to report?" asked First Daughter.

Lucky held his breath.

"We conducted basic tree recognition, ma'am."

"Good—then we shall see you tomorrow."

"Thank you, ma'am." Mazie glared at Lucky as she left.

The next day Lucky tried to thank her.

"Don't be stupid again," she said crossly. "D'you know how much trouble *I'd* be in if First Daughter found out? Don't think I even *like* you!"

"Oh, I know you don't like me," said Lucky.

Mazie was taken aback. "What do you mean?"

"You're only helping me so you can get out of the Foraging ranks. First Daughter told me."

Mazie couldn't help herself; she had to ask. "Did she say anything else?"

"Oh, yes—she said that you're too clever for your own good!"

Mazie shut up—First Daughter was probably right.

The days started to shorten, the leaves turned brown, and the berries ripened. Mazie took Lucky down to Ground-level and showed him the best places to dig under the trees and how to spot the fallen nuts. They worked well together, stuffing their cheeks with the bounty, then taking it back to bury below the roots of the home-trees.

Lucky took extra food back to First Daughter and she was delighted. He had also grown a little more and was quicker in the branches now. But he would have to leave soon—too soon, she thought.

Lucky had learned not to ask why too often—but one thing was starting to puzzle him. So he waited until Mazie was in a fairly good mood and asked, "Mazie, why are all the foragers females?"

He'd expected her to call him stupid straight away—but instead she gestured with her tail for him to follow. They scampered along the safe Mid-level branches until they came to the last six magnificent chestnut trees at the end of the Avenue.

They got to the final chestnut overlooking a big metal gate and the entrance to the Park. "Over there"—Mazie pointed to the trees beyond—"is the Northend!"

He was obviously supposed to be impressed, but all Lucky could see was another avenue of trees that didn't look as tall or as leafy as the Cloudfoots' trees.

"Many years ago the Northenders attacked our Avenue. They raided our stores and stole our food, and many squirrels died." Mazie shook her head sadly. "We weren't prepared. But since then every male trains in Cadet Troop before joining the Watch and Patrol, to guard and defend our Clan. Come on, I'll show you higher up."

They corkscrewed up the chestnut tree and got close to the Canopy. The high, windswept branches had lost most of their leaves; the squirrels were an easy target for the hunting birds. "It's dangerous up here," Mazie reminded him.

Lucky didn't need reminding. He checked for incoming, then looked out over the Northend. No wonder they had wanted to invade! The Northend trees were stunted and thin, bordered by concrete tower blocks. There were no berry-laden bushes at Ground-level and little cover to forage safely. It was a poor habitat compared to the lush Cloudfoot Avenue.

"Do the Northenders still come?" he asked.

"Oh, yes, small raiding parties—our Watch is always looking out and the Patrols deal with any attack."

"But what does that have to do with foraging?" asked Lucky, still puzzled.

"We forage so the males can defend against the Northend threat," explained Mazie. "The Daughter Generals are in charge—well, the Ma's in charge really. We all follow the Word of Ma, it's the law." She looked out toward the trees, a gleam in her beady little eyes. "One day I will be a great Daughter General and plan an attack back!"

"Why can't we be friends with them?"

"You can't be friends with Northenders," snapped Mazie. "They're the enemy."

Lucky felt very foolish; he was never going to understand these Cloudfoots.

"Come on," said Mazie, seeing his unhappy face. "I'll show you the Albion while we're here."

The squirrels scurried to the other side of the tree and Lucky looked down into the Albion restaurant patio below. "Mazie, look at all that food!"

There, among the wooden benches and tables scattered around the patio, was a feast. Bags of potato chips and scatterings of peanuts lay under the tables. There were metal trash cans dotted around, overflowing with tasty things.

"We're not supposed to forage there."

"Why?" asked Lucky, before he could stop himself.

"Because the humans use it."

"But it's empty," said Lucky. "There's no one there at all!"

Mazie scanned the area carefully. He was right—there was no sign of danger and there was a *lot* of food. "No harm in a *little* foraging then," she said, "but we must be very careful."

Lucky didn't need to be told twice. He leapt down the chestnut tree and hopped across the patio at breakneck speed. *First Daughter will be so pleased when I bring this back to the drey*, he thought. He started to scamper from table to table, happily stuffing his cheeks with peanuts. This was wonderful! He moved farther and farther away from the trees with no thought of danger . . .

He was close to the restaurant doors when Mazie's cry of warning reached his ears. He twirled around but couldn't see her. He scanned the garden in alarm—where was she?

A sudden volley of yapping brought him up short and he instinctively jumped onto a table. He was just in time to see Mazie leaping up the nearest tree—with a furious little white dog snapping at her heels. The angry dog ran wildly around the tree trunk, barking manically, his prey safely out of reach. Then he spotted Lucky.

Jock the Westie had spent all his life chasing squirrels. He'd never caught one, but that didn't stop him. He chased anything that moved: birds, cats, and dogs twice his size. He chased them all, yapping and snapping.

"He's only trying to be friendly," said his human. "He just wants to play." But she was kidding herself. Jock didn't want to play—he wanted to *bite*. He was a bad-tempered and thoroughly nasty little West Highland terrier.

"Gotcha, ya wee tree-rat!" yapped Jock in vicious delight as he bounded toward the table.

Lucky spun around desperately, searching for an escape route. The trees were too far away and he was surrounded by an island of tables. Could the little terrier get up onto the table? You bet he could!

Jock jumped nimbly onto the bench and launched himself at Lucky, claws scrabbling and teeth bared. The squirrel dropped to the ground and ran for his life. The Westie leapt after him, still yapping hysterically.

Mazie watched, horrified and helpless, as Lucky skidded around the garden and the dog got closer and closer to his tail. Around and around they raced, dodging in and out of table legs, over and under benches. What was he doing? Why wasn't he running toward the trees?

"Run for the trees!"

But Lucky had no plan; he'd completely lost his head. The trees? *What trees?* Rank dog smell stung his nostrils, the Westie's hot breath on his heels, his snapping teeth and mad yapping filling his ears. *Run! Yes, run!* He ran in blind terror and then—

An explosion of terrible pain—a *smack* between the eyes—stopped him short and Lucky reeled backward and thudded to the ground. He'd run headlong into a metal trash can.

The chase was over. The Westie stood over him, triumphant and sneering.

"Gotcha!" he panted.

4

Finlay

Gotcha!" yapped the delighted little dog again.

"Leave it, Jock," growled a deep voice.

The Westie looked up to see a huge shaggy old German shepherd dog walk slowly into the beer garden.

"No way, Finlay! Ya interfering greet cur!" swore Jock nastily. "It's mine, fair and square—I've waited *years* ta git ma teeth into a squirrel!"

"Leave it, Jock—or I won't be responsible for the consequences," growled Finlay.

"Oh yeah?" The Westie's hackles rose. "Ya want ta make something of it?"

Finlay sighed and moved to one side. An evil-looking

black Staffordshire bull terrier stood behind him, grinning manically and baring his fangs.

"Oh, that's nay fair!" whined Jock peevishly. "Fight me dog ta dog!"

Why, thought Finlay, *are little dogs always so foolishly aggressive?* "I don't want to fight you, Jock," he said. "I keep the peace around here. Just leave the squirrel and go home."

The Westie moved grudgingly away from the limp body of Lucky. "Ya greet coward," he growled, looking up at Finlay, who was four times his size. "I'll have ya—when you've nay got a friend ta back you up!"

"Blimey, Fin, he can't talk to you like that!" spluttered the Staffy. "Let me bite him! Can I bite him? Go on, Fin—just a little nip?"

Finlay shook his head, then turned back to the Westie. "Jock, one of these days some dog's going to call your bluff—and don't expect *me* to help you out."

"Pah!" yapped the terrier and trotted off, furiously muttering curses under his breath.

Finlay gazed down at Lucky, who stared back, rigid with fear. "It's all right, son, we're not going to hurt you. Why aren't you up in the safety of the trees like a sensible young squirrel?"

At that moment Mazie came rushing hysterically up to the dogs. "Eat me!" she cried. "Eat me! I'm much bigger and he'll taste horrible! Look what a funny color he is!" Mazie stood trembling from whisker to tail, tears streaming down her face.

"Don't be dumb," said the Staffy. "We aren't going to eat *you*; you're all skin and bone."

"Eric, this is no time for jokes," said Finlay sternly.

"I'm not joking, Fin," protested Eric. "I tried it once and—"

"Eric, that's enough!"

Finlay looked more closely at Lucky. "I know you! You're the youngster that we found in the Park. We took you to the Ma."

"You know the Ma?" Mazie was horrified—this was getting worse! "Oh, please, please don't tell her we were here! It's all my fault—First Daughter will never forgive me!"

"Now, now, miss," said Finlay. "I've always been a friend to the Cloudfoots. I'm not going to get you into trouble." The dog looked down at Lucky, who was shaking with fear and delayed shock.

More memories were starting to surface. Lucky remembered a soft, warm drey, remembered being torn from it. A terrible noise, blinding light, and falling . . . his mother calling for him . . . crackling feathers and sharp talons . . . being carried up into the sky . . .

And then . . . the Darkness. His teeth started to chatter.

"Let's get him back to the trees, miss; he's had a nasty shock. He's a very lucky squirrel."

"Oh, yes," said Mazie. "I know that!"

They got to the safety of the chestnut tree trunk and Lucky started to calm down. "D-do you know me?" he stuttered, looking up at the huge dog.

"Aye, we've met before," said Finlay, "but you won't remember—"

"'Cause you were 'alf dead!" interrupted Eric.

"You were unconscious—"

"Being as you'd been dropped from the sky by an 'awk!"

An 'awk?

"He means a large hunting bird," said Finlay. "It came down to finish you off—"

"And I bit him!" added the Staffy proudly.

"Eric!"

"Well, I saved him, didn't I? The 'awk flew off!"

"B-but where did I *come* from?" said Lucky.

"Not from these parts of the woods. You're a long way from home."

"How do you know that, Mr. Finlay?" asked Mazie.

"He's a red squirrel, miss. They're very rare, so he must have been taken from a sanctuary out in the countryside."

Lucky had no idea what a "sanctuary" was, but suddenly he was trembling with excitement rather than shock. Of course! He'd been taken from the drey! His mother, his brothers and sisters . . . everything he half remembered from before the Darkness was real!

"So I don't belong here," he declared. "I'm not like the Cloudfoots at all!" He had known this, of course—but he had thought he was on his own. Now he could try and find his own clan!

"Well, you're still a squirrel, son," said Finlay kindly. "If the Cloudfoots dropped in on your home-trees they'd look pretty odd too, but gray or red, you're all squirrels."

"But this isn't my real home!"

"Of course it's your real home!" snapped Mazie. "Where else is there?"

"Well, I could go back to the 'sanctuary' trees," declared Lucky. "I'd be an ordinary squirrel there; I'd be like everyone else!" *And I could see my real mum and family*, he thought, but he didn't like to say it in front of Mazie.

"Son," said Finlay, as gently as he could, "I'm really sorry. You can't ever go home. It's too far. You're just going to have to make the best of it here."

When they returned to the home-tree, First Daughter could tell that there was something wrong, but neither squirrel would admit to a problem.

"Thanks for not telling," said Mazie.

"Oh, that's okay," said Lucky dully. "We'd both have been in trouble."

"Yes, but I wouldn't be allowed to forage with you anymore and . . ." She hesitated and smiled.

Lucky had never seen her smile before.

"And I'd miss that, Lucky squirrel."

5

Northenders

Raised voices could be heard from the Fleet Family drey. It wasn't a grand home, but it was in one of the few good Northend trees. Inside, the Honorable Mistress Tarragon Fleet was determined to get her own way.

"But you promised!"

Major Fleet struggled to keep his temper. This argument had been going on for some time, and he didn't have time to waste. "Tarragon—"

"But, Uncle, you promised! And you're *always* going on about duty and Family—and you *said* I could come out with you today!"

"I have told you, this is not a good day—"

"I don't care!" she wailed. "I'm bored! You *promised* me an outing!"

"Oh, very well," snapped the Major, finally giving in, "but you mustn't—"

"Get-in-the-way! I know!"

"And you must—"

"Obey-your-commands-at-all-times," chanted Tarragon, skipping around the drey in triumph. "Ooh-ooh, I'm so excited now!"

The Major gritted his teeth. Fighting any rival Northend Family was easier than dealing with this foolish young female!

"Ooh-ooh, can we go and spy on the enemy Cloudfoots?" Tarragon shuddered in delight at the terrifying prospect.

"Niece, have you not listened to a word I've said? A foraging party went into the Towers at dawn. The sun is almost at the Mid-levels so I must be at our boundary trees to meet them, and I am late."

Tarragon didn't care—it was all just so exciting! "Ooh-ooh, goody!" She jumped up and down. "Let's go!"

Major Fleet controlled many of the Northend trees, but not enough to keep every squirrel under his rule well fed— there were simply too many feuding Families, and the Major had temporary alliances with some, and uneasy truces with others.

Many smaller, lesser Families only occupied one or two trees, and fights for food and territory broke out all the time. *One day*, thought the Major, as they scurried toward the boundary trees, *I will find a way to unite this rabble—and then what a force the Northend will be!*

As they passed small groups of Fleet squirrels in adjoining branches, Tarragon waved enthusiastically at her Family. "Hello! How are you?" she signaled with her tail.

The common Fleet squirrels, deeply embarrassed that they had been noticed by the Honorable Mistress, bobbed low and made clumsy gestures of reply. They tried not to catch the Major's eye.

"Tarragon," he snapped, "we're not here for you to stop and gossip."

"Yes, Uncle," she said meekly. She could see he was cross now, and it didn't do to anger the Major—even she knew that. But it was so unfair! She never got to talk to anyone outside the drey. *When I'm older*, she thought, *I'm going to go out every day and speak to whoever I like—and no one's going to stop me!*

The dirty crumbling Towers came into sight and Tarragon shuddered. *How can humans live in there?* she thought. *They're not proper trees at all, and the humans don't even use the viewing platforms. No leaf cover—nothing grows up the trunks—they're horrible!*

Tarragon was right: The old concrete tower blocks had tiny balconies and had been built to cram in as many humans as possible. The only garden was a small strip of grass at the front, which was always covered in litter. Only sad dogs, stuck in the Towers with their humans, used it—and they used it as a toilet.

Despite its ugly look, however, every Northender knew that behind the Towers was a great prize: huge trash cans overflowing with food, thrown away by the wasteful humans. When the trash cans were full, there were also plastic sacks to forage through, piled high. It was a place of plenty amid the barren concrete, and if you kept a wary eye out for foxes, it was like squirrel snacking heaven.

But today there was no sign of the foraging party. The six soldiers should have returned by now, so where were they?

There was a busy road between the trees and the Towers, and the foul fumes of the humans' metal boxes drifted up into the Mid-levels. The squirrels went as far out onto an overhanging branch as they dared, and Tarragon spotted a little gray shape far below, limping toward the road.

"Uncle, look!"

The squirrel was going as fast as he could and leapt out

into the traffic, dodging awkwardly between the cars. For a moment it looked like he might make it—then a car came straight at him.

"Oh, no!"

Tarragon didn't want to look. Most humans would run straight over a squirrel, either because they didn't see them or because they didn't care. But this Northender was lucky. The human driving her young to school spotted him just in time, and with a squeal of brakes she swerved.

"Ooh-ooh, goody, he got to the trees!" Tarragon clapped in delight.

Tooth and claw! thought the Major. *The silly child thinks it's all a game!* He spiraled quickly down the tree. Something was wrong. Where were the rest of his troops?

Something *was* wrong, and Tarragon let out a gasp of surprise when they were close enough to see the soldier. Blood was dripping down his haunches. No wonder he was limping—he had been badly bitten.

"Report, Corporal!" ordered the Major.

"Sir!" The male staggered, trying to salute.

Tarragon was horrified. "Uncle, he's hurt—can't we get help?"

"Don't interfere, girl, I need to know what happened."

"Rats," gasped the injured corporal. "Swarms of them. Th-they ambushed us."

"What! You didn't smell them?"

"N-no, sir! They were . . . in the bins." He shuddered. "They waited until we were close to the food and poured out of the bins. No noise—they made no noise but kept on coming, more and more. W-we fought and—they *just kept coming*!"

"Pull yourself together, Corporal! Where is the rest of the troop?"

The soldier looked wretched. "They're all gone—th-they didn't stand a chance!"

"So how did *you* manage to escape?" asked the Major coldly.

The young corporal could hardly look him in the face. "They captured me, sir."

"What!"

"Their Rat Lord wanted me t-to deliver a m-message, sir," whispered the miserable squirrel. "I didn't want to!"

Bud and branch, thought Tarragon, *this is horrible. I've never seen Uncle look so angry. Surely it's not the corporal's fault?*

"Well, what is this message?" he growled.

"The Rat Lord proclaims all of the Towers his territory now. B-but if the Northenders wanted to send him m-more squirrel meat . . . he . . . he'd be happy to have it."

Tarragon grabbed the Major's arm as he went to strike the corporal. "Uncle, he's injured—it's not his fault!"

"Fault! I will Cast you Down, you miserable coward!"

"I didn't want to do it, sir! I begged them not to send me back. The Rat Lord just laughed at me. I know—I know I have dishonored you . . . Cast me Down now!"

"No!" cried Tarragon, leaping between them. "This is silly! Five soldiers are dead—why lose another?"

"Because he surrendered!"

"But if he hadn't brought the message back, you would have sent more soldiers to the Towers," reasoned Tarragon. "Then they'd have been attacked too."

The Major stopped; amazingly, the female had a point. "Very well. But hear this, Corporal. You have been spared only by Mistress Tarragon's intervention—for now."

The injured corporal nodded dumbly and the Major swept Tarragon away.

Back in the home-tree, Tarragon found she was shaking. Her drey companion scurried up, eager for news. But Tarragon realized she didn't want to talk about it. She'd wanted excitement, but it had been horrible—and squirrels from her Family had *died*. It hadn't been the corporal's fault, but he had wanted to die too, because of some silly invisible thing called "honor." It was all too complicated and confusing, so she crept into her moss-bed and slept.

She felt better when she woke. It had been exciting *really*, hadn't it? She had just decided to tell the story after all, when word came that she had a visitor.

"You won't want to see her, mistress," said her companion. "She is something of a scrub. A shoddy creature, from a coarse branch of the Family. I don't think the Major would like you to—"

"Don't be silly. I never get any visitors. Send her in!"

The gray squirrel who shuffled nervously into the drey was skinny and very old. *But that's no reason to call her a scrub*, thought Tarragon. *And she looks terrified.*

The old female made a stiff bob and held out a parcel of leaves in her shaking paws.

"For me?" Tarragon opened the parcel. Inside were a few dried and wrinkled berries, and Tarragon could hear her companion snickering behind her. She ignored her and made a polite tail gesture of thanks.

"What can I do for you, Grandmother?"

"Oh, no, mistress, this is a gift of thanks—from the corporal's wife. We are all so grateful for what you did. It was very brave."

"Ooh-ooh, how nice!"

"Oh, my! You sound just like your dear departed mother—" The old squirrel stopped, suddenly flustered.

"Thank you," Tarragon said softly. "I don't really remember her, or my father. But the Major said they were both very brave."

The old squirrel gave her a very strange look. "May you store and survive, mistress," she stuttered, as the companion bustled her out of the drey.

She's frightened, thought Tarragon. *What does she have to be frightened about?*

6

Amber

Finlay wagged his tail in thanks as his human let him out of the house. Tail-wagging was an easy way to reward humans and Finlay liked to encourage George—he was a good human, and they had been working together in the Force for many years. But when the old detective had had to retire, so had Finlay.

It's ridiculous, thought the German shepherd. *I'm only twelve years old. In my prime! I should get another partner.* But he had stuck by George—you couldn't just abandon humans, not when you'd had them all your life.

George didn't seem to like retirement much either, and he spent all his time slumped in front of the TV watching the Serious Crime Channel. Fortunately, the human understood that Finlay wanted to carry on patrolling, and let him out every evening. "Scratch at the door when you want to come in!" called George, as Finlay trotted down the garden path. He always said that—Finlay had him very well trained.

The German shepherd padded along Park Road with the familiar feel of paving stones beneath his huge paws. "Chill in the air," sniffed the old dog. "Definite smell of autumn."

The distant roar of traffic and trains running into the city never stopped. But Finlay's ears were pricked for other noises—a dog in distress, or a fight to break up. Cats were wailing and calling in the backyards and alleys, but Finlay ignored them—the local top tom would deal with any trouble in his territory, and the dog wasn't going to interfere in cat business.

But he would stop a silly young pup from chasing a cat. At best, the thrill of pursuit could get a dog lost. At worst, if a cat turned to fight, razor-sharp claws dragged deep down the nose were *not* nice.

All seemed peaceful as dusk settled and the streetlights started to come on. *I wonder if Eric's in*, Finlay thought, and he turned down Manor Road and went to the back of number 47. The gate wasn't locked—it didn't need to be, as no sane human would break in with Eric in the yard.

The demonic-looking Staffordshire bull terrier was actually a very softhearted animal. But he had a bad-boy reputation to keep up for his human, Roadkill, who was always getting into fights. No one would dare touch the pierced and tattooed biker with Eric by his side, and the dog could repel trouble with a snarl. He also didn't mind acting like a deranged maniac for the human, though he did object to Roadkill calling him "Satan"—it was just *wrong*.

Finlay raised the latch of the gate and went into Eric's yard. The Staffy had already smelled his friend coming and was wagging his stumpy tail in greeting.

"Evening, Eric, want to come—"

Finlay stopped in surprise. Eric was wearing a brand-new leather harness that was covered in shiny studs and spikes; the legend "Satan" was engraved on the breastplate.

"I see Roadkill's got you a—"

"Don't wanna talk about it, Fin," muttered the Staffy unhappily.

"That's, um, quite understandable," said Finlay, trying to keep a straight face. "I just wondered if you fancied coming on patrol with me?"

"Yeah," sighed Eric. "I need to get out."

They trotted up the road side by side. Although the Staffy only came up to the old German shepherd's shoulders, every bit of him was solid muscle. Eric was the best backup any dog could have, but teaching him policing wasn't easy.

"Biting first and asking questions later is *not* the way we do it in the Force!" It was very hard to get Eric to remember this.

But he was useful. Eric had fearlessly driven the hawk away from the lucky little squirrel that day in the Park. He was fast too; nothing on four legs could outrun Eric.

"We goin' to the Albion?" asked the Staffy.

"Yes, but I thought we'd just stop by the shops and see how Millie the Mutt is getting on. Her human's not well."

"A dog shouldn't 'ave an 'omeless 'uman," sniffed Eric. "It's not right, just 'avin a sleeping bag in a shop doorway."

"Eric, you're being judgmental!"

"Me? Nah! I blooming hate judges; Roadkill says they should all be put down."

I bet he does, thought Finlay.

As they rounded the corner of Main Street, a piercing shriek came from the alley of Mr. Tang's Magic Kitchen. A massive crash and clatter of rolling garbage bin lids was followed by manic yapping. The dogs leapt into action as out of the alley shot a small red-brown shape.

"Follow that fox!" ordered Finlay.

Eric didn't need to be told twice, and he took off like a bullet.

From the terrible noise, Finlay expected a pack of dogs to come dashing out of the alley, but there was only one: Jock, the West Highland terrier.

"Outta ma way!" yapped Jock, trying to get past Finlay. "I'm gonna lose her!"

"Too late, Jock, she's gone, and you've no right harassing innocent animals."

"Innocent? That wee cur is a filthy thief! You should be after her yerself!"

"Okay, Jock, I will, but you go home now. You'll get into trouble messing with foxes."

"I'm no' afraid of foxes!" declared the little dog, but he turned tail and trotted off.

Finlay followed Eric as fast as he could. There was only one direction they could be headed in, and that was to the Park. The Albion gates were at the crossroads, and Finlay thought the fox had probably gone to ground by now. But to his surprise, when he reached the Albion, he found that Eric had apprehended the runaway. The little fox was cowering by the metal gates with the Staffy towering over her.

"I've not bitten her, Fin," said Eric proudly. "I thought you'd want to ask questions first."

"Good work, Eric. Now, miss, what d'you think you're playing at?"

The vixen looked fiercely up at him and did her best to snarl; it came out as a squeak.

Blood and bone! She's just a cub, thought Finlay. *She shouldn't be out of her home-den at night.* "What's your name, young lady?"

"What's it to you?" snapped the cub, not so scared now.

"Does your mother know you're out?"

"Does yours?" said the fox cub, getting cocky. She'd been frightened of the black dog dressed in spikes and leather, but this big one seemed like a soft touch.

"Right, that's it," said Finlay, losing patience. "We're taking you home."

"No! No, it's okay, I can go home on my own." The fox looked genuinely worried now.

Ah, thought Finlay, *she'll be in trouble with her mother if we take her back.* "And where *is* home, Miss . . . ?"

"Amber," said the cub. "I'm Amber. It's just down the road. I'll be okay—honest."

"Well, Miss Amber, we're not going to stop you, but I'd leave the garbage in the main street alone if I were you, and keep close to your home-den. Are you listening to me?"

Amber's eyes snapped back to the dog. "Oh, yeah, yeah," she lied. "What *is* this place?" She gestured to the Park.

"This, Miss Amber, is a dangerous place that a fox cub should keep well away from," said Finlay sternly.

"I can smell some great stuff!"

"Squirrel," said Eric. "Well 'ard to catch."

"Eric! We're *friends* to the squirrels—we do not hunt them." Finlay looked at the fox cub. "Amber, we saved you from that dog at the bins. He's not fussy about who he bites, so I want you to *promise* to keep out of trouble, and that means keeping well away from the Park—and no hunting squirrels!"

"Yeah, yeah, okay," muttered Amber. She was lying. All foxes lied—they couldn't help it.

7

Cadet Troop

Lucky spring-boarded from the tip of a thin branch and flew through the air with his tail flicking and whirring like a propeller.

"Wheeee!"

He landed nimbly on the next branch tip, which bent with his weight, then sprang up, catapulting him outward again. *I'm flying!* "Mazie, look, I'm flying!"

She watched him leaping nimbly from branch to branch, and hid a smile. *He nearly beat me to the home-tree this time*, she thought. *I must let First Daughter know.*

They arrived together, with Lucky out of breath but triumphant. "Did you see that? Bet you can't do that!"

"Don't get cocksure, Lucky squirrel," she said sternly. "Pride goes before a Falling." But secretly she was proud too.

"First Daughter!" called Lucky as they went into the drey. "I got back without touching the tree trunks! Not even once!"

"Well done, my son, I'm very pleased."

She doesn't look very pleased, thought Mazie. *Have I done something wrong?*

"I have something to tell you both," said First Daughter. "I met with the Trial Instructor today and it is agreed. Lucky will join the Cadet Troop at the next full moon."

So soon! Lucky could hardly contain his excitement. "That's great! Isn't that great, Mazie?"

She nodded. "Yes. Yes, of course it is. Congratulations."

Lucky couldn't understand why neither of them looked very happy. But there wasn't much time before the new troop started training, and although Mazie had watched with satisfaction as Lucky became stronger and faster in the trees, she knew that it wasn't enough. And it was too late now.

So in their last remaining days together she taught him the diving skills that her mother had taught her—the diving skills so useful for a quick escape. Mazie had a bad feeling that Lucky might need them . . .

First Daughter also briefed him carefully just before he left on how to behave like a Cloudfoot.

"Always obey the Trial Instructor and *never* make a fuss or complain," she advised. "Watch what the others do and try your best to be like them, but if you can't, find a way that works for *you*."

Lucky nodded solemnly, though this was the third time she'd told him this.

"Remember to judge the terrain," First Daughter continued. "The first and most obvious move might not be the best. *Think*, Lucky. Use your head—"

"And be careful!" interrupted Mazie. First Daughter's whiskers stiffened in disapproval and the young squirrel hurriedly shut up.

Lucky nodded again and stuck his head out of the drey. Then, with a deep breath, he launched himself down the home-tree to the training branches below.

The two females watched him go. "Good-speed, Lucky," whispered Mazie.

"Good-speed indeed," said First Daughter. "And now, Miss Trimble, I shall not need your services as tutor anymore."

"Of course, ma'am," said Mazie miserably. "Lucky won't have time to forage now."

"Neither will you, Miss Trimble," said First Daughter briskly. "I want you to move into my home-tree immediately. It's time you were promoted."

Lucky hurried down the trunk. He mustn't be late. This was the big day! *I'll show them*, he thought determinedly. *If I'm stuck in these trees, then I'll show them I can be as good as any Cloudfoot!*

But he was a little bit worried. Mazie had never let him meet any of the other young squirrels. What would they be like?

He landed lightly on a branch near another group of males and was immediately surrounded. They all pushed and shoved to get a closer look.

"It's the lucky squirrel!"

"Wow! Your ears really are weird!"

"We've heard all about you!"

They chattered around him, fascinated, friendly, and full of questions. Lucky tried his best to answer, overwhelmed by the attention.

Yes, he'd always been this color. No, he hadn't had an accident; of course they were his real ears! Yes, he knew he was smaller than them—but he was still growing!

Only one squirrel held back, and Lucky recognized him—the big sullen male he'd seen with Second Daughter. "He's not going to grow," sneered the squirrel. "He's just a runt."

"Shut up, Nimlet," said one of the males.

"Yes, shut it," said another. "Take no notice of him, Lucky."

"No one likes him."

"Not even his mother likes him!" declared the first squirrel. The Cloudfoot males rolled around laughing at this display of wit.

"I'm sure she does," said Lucky, feeling a bit sorry for Nimlet now.

"Don't even *talk* about my mother!" threatened Nimlet. "Or I'll—"

"Troop!" A stern voice cut through the air. "I expect silence and attention from my cadets and I shall have both—*now*!"

The chatter stopped dead and Lucky saw a grizzled sharp-faced male moving slowly toward them. Surely this small scraggy squirrel wasn't the Trial Instructor? First Daughter had told him that the Instructor was a great warrior. *That must have been a long time ago*, he thought. *This squirrel's* really *old*.

"Now," said the Trial Instructor, glaring at them and plainly not liking what he saw. "You are all here because you want to join the Watch and Patrol."

The squirrels all nodded obediently.

"But what you want, gentlemen," he continued drily, "does not come without commitment and hard work. There will be training, there will be trials, and no Cloudfoot joins the Watch and Patrol unless he can pass the Final Run. And if he does not pass . . . ?" He left the question hanging in the air.

"He will be Cast Down!" chorused all the males except Lucky. What did the old squirrel mean?

"Correct," continued the Instructor. "Cast Down to the Ground-level and banished from the Cloudfoot trees— forever!"

Lucky suddenly realized why First Daughter and Mazie had been so unhappy. Cadet Troop was a one-way branch, and they were worried that he'd fail the Final Run. *I'm* not *going to fail*, he thought. *I'm going to make them proud*.

"We have a fine tradition to uphold, gentlemen," continued the Trial Instructor. "My great-great-great-grandfather started the Watch and Patrol . . ."

"I bet he looked like a rat too!" whispered the witty squirrel.

"Cadet!" snapped the old male—clearly there was nothing wrong with his hearing. Several squirrels moved fractionally away from the unfortunate youngster. "Cadet, do you think *you* could defend our Avenue like our brave forefathers did at the Battle of the New Dawn?"

The squirrel trembled; he was not so witty now. "Y-yes, sir!"

"Really? Well, sadly we do not have a horde of attacking Northenders in the trees." The other males realized this was supposed to be a joke and tittered nervously. "So we shall just have to see if you can get past *me*." The Instructor beckoned the horrified squirrel over to his branch.

"I—I don't want to hurt you, sir!" The young cadet was a sleek, strong male who towered over the Instructor.

"Indeed," said the old male in his dry voice. "But all you need to do is get past me to the trunk." He beckoned the very worried-looking youngster forward again and crouched slowly down on his haunches.

There was a blur of flying fur as the young squirrel lunged forward and was flipped, tackled, and tossed in the air by the old male. Grabbing his tail, the Instructor whirled him around his head and slammed him down on the branch with a *thud*!

How did he do that? The young male lay spread-eagled and groaning.

"That," announced the Trial Instructor crisply, "was a demonstration of the tail-throw. A useful move against a larger and less intelligent opponent." He bent down to pull the stunned youngster to his feet. "Call me a 'rat' again, Cadet," he said calmly, "and your mother will wish you'd never left the drey."

"Yes, sir," mumbled the humiliated male.

"Now, let's see if *any* of the rest of you rabble are Cloudfoot material . . ."

8

Tag

S o, gentlemen," the Trial Instructor began, "the first exercise is a *simple* little game."

I don't believe it, thought Lucky. *There's going to be a catch in here somewhere.* The other squirrels looked worried too.

"You may know the game as 'tag.' While playing it, you will familiarize yourselves with the Mid-level runs."

All the squirrels brightened up—this was going to be fun!

"The exercise is designed to build up your strength, speed, and stamina," the Trial Instructor continued. "So you will chase and tag your partner, then return to me at base to repeat the operation. You will play until sunset, gentlemen, and I shall be watching."

The squirrels groaned. Nonstop tag? All day? This wasn't going to be fun at all . . .

The Instructor started to pair off the cadets. At the last group of squirrels his eyes narrowed when he saw Lucky and Nimlet.

Tooth and claw! The strange red squirrel was clearly a weakling, and Nimlet was known to be shortsighted and clumsy. He could show no favoritism here, even if they were the sons of First and Second Daughter. But he might need to give them some extra help outside class or they'd both fail.

"Mr. Nimlet, Mr. Lucky, you will be tag mates."

"But, sir—"

"Are you presuming to argue with me, Mr. Nimlet?"

Nimlet bristled with rage, his tail flicking furiously. You didn't question the Trial Instructor, but why pair him with this loser? "No, sir!"

"Then get moving, Cadet."

Yes, thought Nimlet, gritting his teeth. *I'll move all right. That spiky-eared scrub won't stand a chance against me!*

Each squirrel that was "it" was given a horse chestnut. The nut casing was covered in tiny hooked burrs that attached easily to body- or tail-fur. His tag mate was given a few minutes' start, and then the chase was on. They had to tag their partners by attaching the horse chestnut and then get back to base before they were tagged back.

The Trial Instructor handed out the chestnuts and Nimlet shoved theirs into Lucky's paws.

"You're *it*," he said bluntly and crashed through the tree growth, disappearing from view before the starting signal.

Lucky looked around, completely confused. *I mustn't start before the others*, he thought, remembering First Daughter's advice. He held the chestnut firmly between his teeth and, at the Instructor's signal, took off after Nimlet.

Loser! thought Nimlet as he furiously blundered through the branches. *He'll never catch me. Strength and stamina? Huh! I'm stronger than him any day.* He hurled himself from tree to tree, recklessly careering up the Avenue.

Then he had an idea. *I can outrun him* and *outleap him! I'll go up to the Canopy, and he won't even know where to look!* So he headed to the higher levels, where the branches thinned out and the distance between the trees became wider and more difficult to cross.

The sound of laughter and the chase of the other tag partners drifted away as Nimlet climbed. "Mustn't get too high," he panted. "Dangers in the Canopy." He stopped and squinted at the sky. He might be shortsighted but he wasn't stupid, so he checked the airways. No sign of birds—he was safe. He traveled farther up, leaping vertically from one branch to another. He'd like to see that useless weakling climb like this!

The sunlight was blinding as Nimlet reached the top of the trees and the open expanse of sky. He stopped to see if Lucky was following. Good! No sign of the loser! Now all he needed to do was jump onto the topmost branches of the next tree and work his way quietly down to the Mid-levels. Lucky would never find him. Just a little bit farther should do it . . . and Nimlet leapt.

Lucky was halfway up the trunk, following Nimlet's clumsy trail of bent and broken twigs. *I'll never catch him*, he thought, *but at least he's easy to track*. He stopped to catch his breath.

A high-pitched scream suddenly cut through the air. Lucky's head snapped up to see a squirrel crashing down from the next tree. It was Nimlet, falling, twisting and turning with his limbs flailing desperately as he tried to grab on to a branch. Any branch!

Lucky catapulted through the air to the next tree and hit the branch tip as Nimlet tumbled past him. The branch bowed and Lucky made a wild grab for the squirrel. He lurched downward and managed to grasp his tail, just in time. He hung on to the creaking branch as they swung wildly back and forth. *Tooth and claw! I'm going to drop him*, thought Lucky. *He's too heavy!*

Nimlet came to his senses and climbed over Lucky onto the branch. They slowly crawled back to the safety of the tree trunk and Nimlet turned to discover the horse chestnut firmly attached to his fur.

"You're *it*!" said Lucky smugly.

Nimlet was speechless. He looked at the chestnut, and he looked at Lucky. Then he looked at the chestnut again. He looked down through the branches to the ground far below and shuddered. The runt had saved his life!

"Th . . . that was . . . that was . . . completely awesome!" he finally spluttered.

"You're still *it*," said Lucky doggedly.

"Yeah, and I'm still alive!" said Nimlet, grinning. He slapped Lucky on the back, sending the squirrel staggering. "Want to play some more?"

They finished the run side by side, giggling and passing the horse chestnut back and forth in a furious game of catch and run. They tumbled down toward the Mid-levels, somersaulting and leapfrogging over each other. Laughing hysterically, they landed at the starting branch, happily trading insults.

The Trial Instructor was furious that they weren't taking the exercise seriously and failed them both. But who cared?

Lucky had a real friend.

Nimlet had a real friend.

What did anything else matter?

9

Tarragon

The Honorable Mistress Tarragon Fleet stamped her foot. "I *will* go out!"

"Mistress, I really don't think you should—"

"Don't tell me what I can and can't do!" She stamped her foot again.

"But, mistress, the Major said—"

"I don't care," said Tarragon stubbornly. "I'm going out! You don't have to come with me."

"But I'm your companion, mistress!"

"Ooh-ooh, you're so annoying!" Her long-suffering companion looked stricken, and Tarragon felt a twinge of guilt. "Oh, all right," she said, flicking her tail prettily, "you can go and ask the Major for permission to leave the drey."

The female let out a sigh of relief. The Major would be furious if Tarragon was left to discover the Northend on her own. Who knew what she might learn?

"You *will* wait here for me, mistress?" she asked.

"Of course," said Tarragon, smiling her sweetest smile. "I'm not going out on my *own*, am I?" But as the flustered companion left the drey, this was exactly what Tarragon was planning to do.

Going out was so . . . nice! Ever since she'd heroically rescued the corporal, the common squirrels waved and clapped whenever she passed. They liked her! They called out her name, and shoved their young forward to see the Honorable Mistress. Tarragon was delighted and waved back enthusiastically. They did seem to go quiet when the Major glared at them, but of course, he was there to protect her.

She stuck her nose out of the drey to make sure her companion had really gone, then arched gracefully out onto the home-tree branches. It was nearly dusk, but there'd still be a few folk around. She'd go and talk to them.

Or she'd go to the Albion and spot some enemy Cloudfoots. Ooh-ooh, that would be exciting! Hadn't her uncle said something about planning a raid with the Coppice Family? He might even be gathering the Northend troops for action. That would be a marvelous sight to see!

Whiskers quivering in anticipation, the Honorable Mistress Tarragon Fleet went out to explore.

Amber the fox cub never stamped her foot, or asked permission to leave the den. She just went out, whatever her mother said.

Headstrong, the old vixen thought. *Never had a cub this reckless. Trouble, that's what she is.*

But Amber didn't want to get into trouble; she just wanted to have her own way. Somehow, trouble tracked her down.

As Tarragon was leaving her drey in the Northend, Amber was emerging from her city den into the dusk. A pale crescent moon was rising above the distant tower blocks and human and other animal sounds mingled with the distant roar of the traffic. Amber could taste wood smoke in the air and the tantalizing smells of scurrying small night prey. *Good hunting!* she thought. *But first, a snack at one of the bins.*

She realized that Mr. Tang's Magic Kitchen attracted too much competition. There was the nasty little white dog, and sometimes bigger stray dogs, really desperate for food. Cats she could deal with, but then there were also the rats, and she'd rather *not* deal with them—too many teeth in a rat pack, and far too nasty.

No, Mr. Tang's Magic Kitchen was too much trouble—and she'd found a much easier source of food in the backyard trash cans along Park Road. She'd also found bowls of food, put out by the humans for their cats.

Amber was a clever thief and could smell a cat coming from streets away. She also knew that if you held your nerve in a cat face-off they'd back down. They could hiss and puff up their fur all they liked, but she still stole their food.

She stealthily trotted down the road and slipped under the gate to the first backyard. It was empty and the garbage bin lids were firmly closed. *I'll try farther up*, she thought, and leapt over the wall.

Spud the mongrel was asleep in his kennel, snoring loudly. He was dreaming of cats and it was a good dream. He chomped his massive jaws on imaginary tails, and cries for mercy went unheeded. Then a whiff of rank fox hit his nose, and he slowly opened an eye.

Amber knew there was a dog in the little wooden den. But there was also a big juicy bone on the lawn, and she was sure the dog was asleep.

She was wrong! Spud exploded out of the kennel in a rage. "Mine! Mine!" he slavered madly. Amber turned tail and ran frantically for the backyard wall, when a rattle of a chain and a *snap* made her turn. The dog was straining pop-eyed against a leash, his teeth gnashing and foam flying from his jaws. "Mine! Mine! My bone!"

"Nah-ha! Can't catch me!" taunted Amber, and she leapt nimbly over the wall. That had been close!

She ran swiftly through the next yards and suddenly realized she was nearly at the Albion. She'd promised the old police dog not to go back there. Huh! She headed for the Park . . .

Tarragon had been right—there were a few Northend squirrels in the trees, but they were hurrying home as night drew in. *Never mind*, she thought, *I will go to the Albion. I'll go and spy on the Cloudfoots! I don't care* what *Uncle says.*

She headed for the Park . . .

Back in the Northend drey, the Major loomed over the cowering form of Tarragon's companion. "You were ordered *never* to leave her alone," he growled.

"M-Mistress Tarragon promised to stay here, sir—"

Thwack! She was slammed against the drey wall, where she reeled from the Major's blow.

"Get out," he spat. "I'll deal with you later."

The hurt and terrified squirrel ran crying from the drey.

The Major paced up and down furiously. *Tooth and claw! I don't need this distraction*, he thought. *Gone to the Albion, I know it in my bones. If she alerts the Cloudfoots to my raid, I'll skin her alive! The Coppice Family have only just agreed to join me. Any excuse and they'll turn tail. I have to find her—and quickly.*

The Albion gates were well lit by streetlights, but the huge chestnut trees at the start of Cloudfoot Avenue were deep in shadow. Tarragon strained to see any squirrels in the dark branches. Nothing! How disappointing.

Her eye was caught by a shape swiftly moving across the gates. *Ooh-ooh, what's that?* She spiraled down the tree trunk to get a better view. Was it a dog? No, it didn't look like a dog—she knew what dogs looked like. What a lovely bushy tail it had!

Amber spotted the small gray shape coming down the tree and smiled slyly. Good hunting! But how to get to the prey?

Tarragon stopped on the lowest branches and waved. "Hello! You're not a dog, are you?"

Amber couldn't believe her luck. How stupid could a squirrel be? "Hiya," she said brightly, grinning upward. "Can't see you up there, come a bit closer."

Tarragon scurried farther down the trunk. *Not close enough*, thought Amber. "You don't look like a dog," the squirrel said.

"Come down and you'll see better," Amber called. The foolish squirrel moved closer, still just out of reach. "I'm just like a dog. I'm a . . . *friend* of the squirrels. A friend . . . like Mr. Finlay."

As Tarragon came farther down, Amber's mouth began watering. Now the prey was in reach!

"Ooh-ooh, how exciting!" Even Tarragon had heard of the famous police dog. "Do you know Mr. Finlay? I'd *love* to meet him!"

"Yes, Northender, she knows Mr. Finlay," said the old dog, stepping out of the shadows. Tarragon's mouth fell open. He was huge!

"What are *you* doing here?" snapped Amber.

"Waiting for you, young lady. I knew you'd be back. And what did I tell you about hunting squirrels?"

"Wasn't going to hurt it," lied Amber.

"Oh, just wanted to be *friends*, did we?"

"Yeah! That's it! Honest!"

Finlay sighed. "Amber, if I ever find you hunting squirrel again you're going to regret it."

"Oh, yeah? You going to *make* me regret it?" she said cockily.

"No, not me—but I might let Eric bite first and ask questions later." Amber looked worried—she didn't want to cross the Staffy. "So go home this instant!" barked Finlay crossly, and she trotted sullenly away. "Now, miss," he said, turning to Tarragon, "there are a few things you need to know about foxes."

At that moment the Major came bounding down the tree toward them. "Tarragon! I've been worried sick. My thanks, Finlay, you've found her safe. The Northend is in your debt. Come, niece, we must go home at once." He started to drag her back up the tree.

"But, Uncle, I want to know about the foxes! And I want to talk to Mr. Finlay . . ."

"Come now"—he smiled through gritted teeth—"before I lose my temper."

He bustled Tarragon through the branches in a silent rage and shoved her into the drey, where an unfamiliar, stern-faced female was waiting for them.

"Who's this?"

"Juniper. Your new companion," snapped the Major.

"But I don't need a new companion," wailed Tarragon. "I've already got a companion!"

"Not anymore," said the Major grimly.

10

Patrolling

Nimlet squinted across the wide windswept void to the next Cloudfoot tree and shook his head. "You'll never make it."

"Want to bet?" challenged Lucky.

"It's too far. No one uses this route—there's a better path on the lower levels."

"Watch me, I've done this before!" declared Lucky, and he started to claw up the tree bark.

"Hey! You said you could jump it from this branch!"

"Just watch me, Nim!" shouted Lucky from above. "And keep back by the trunk!" He looked down at the thin branch below and then across to the tree. This was a long leap, longer than he'd ever done with Mazie. He'd boasted he could do it. Now . . . he wasn't so sure. *Good-speed*, he thought, *that's all I need . . .*

Bud and branch! thought Nimlet, as Lucky dove from the branch above and sped down toward him. *He's nuts!*

Lucky hit the target, bowing down the branch, then shot up with a *twang* and launched into the air. Nimlet held his breath as Lucky sailed through the air and landed on the faraway tree. He spun around dramatically and waved to Nimlet in triumph.

Spiky-eared show-off, thought Nimlet. *If he can do it, so can I!* He started to climb. *I see how it's done. Drop, bounce, push off—easy!*

Lucky was waving frantically at him now. *Yeah, go on— wave,* thought Nimlet peevishly. *I'm coming to your branch sooner than you think!* He took a deep breath and plunged down the tree.

Lucky stopped waving; it was too late to stop his friend now. He watched in horror as the big squirrel dropped like a stone toward a branch that was far too thin. "No! Not that branch—it's going to—"

Break. The branch bent flat against the trunk with a *thwack*, and the wood split at the spar. Nimlet splattered facedown onto the bark, his limbs splayed and tail drooping. Lucky hurried back across to the stunned and angry squirrel.

"Go on," said Nimlet, crossly spitting out pieces of bark. "You know you want to."

"What?" asked Lucky innocently.

"Say 'I told you so'!"

"No, I wasn't going to say that!"

"What did I do wrong?" asked Nimlet, pulling himself stiffly off the trunk.

"Oh, *you* were fine—it was the branch that was, er . . . too thin."

"You mean *I'm* too fat," growled Nimlet.

"No—you're getting fitter," said Lucky quickly. "You're getting muscles. Muscles are heavy."

"Thicker branch?"

Lucky nodded. "A thicker, *stronger* branch."

They scurried down the tree, searching, until Lucky found a likely spot below them.

He pointed down. "That one looks okay."

"It had better be okay," muttered Nimlet. He gathered his strength and dove down the tree again. This time the branch catapulted him like a missile over the ground far below. He landed on the target tree with a *thud* and stood on his hind legs punching the air in delight. Yes!

Can't stop him now, thought Lucky, and he was right. Nimlet wanted another turn at once. Soon they were scuttling up and down the trees, finding target branches and leaping across the void, whooping wildly. Until—

"Cadets!" Lucky and Nimlet stopped in horror. *Ratter!*

Of course they didn't call him Ratter to his face. But after the "call me a 'rat'" episode, all a cadet had to do was mouth "rat" and the troop cracked up. The Instructor was both feared and admired—he *had* to have a nickname.

"Mr. Lucky, Mr. Nimlet, you are *supposed* to be conducting Patrolling Exercises."

Lucky and Nimlet hung their heads guiltily. They should have been at a Watch Point ages ago.

"This is not the Patrol Route, is it, gentlemen?" The squirrels shook their heads in shame. "This is not a game. Patrolling must be taken seriously. You are not supposed to be larking about in the trees!"

Nimlet snorted. Larking?

"But we are taking it seriously, sir!" said Lucky quickly. "We've found some really good new routes!"

"New routes?" spat Ratter in disgust. "There are *no* 'new routes.' The Patrol is a fixed path, every spar, every branch, every Watch Point! Timing, gentlemen! A correctly performing Patrol Group has the whole Avenue under constant observation."

The squirrels shuffled uncomfortably, their eyes cast down.

"Call yourselves Cloudfoots?" snapped Ratter, losing patience. "Return to base immediately."

They followed him obediently back through the trees. "Call me a rat," mouthed Nimlet, and Lucky had a fit of coughing.

As they neared base, the Trial Instructor stiffened, then started to hurry his pace. There was something wrong; there was too much activity in the branches. The chattering news came to them quickly. A raid—a Northend raid!

"Stay here," ordered Ratter, and he leapt off toward the Albion.

"We staying?" asked Nimlet.

"No chance!" said Lucky.

Keeping low, they followed behind, but were soon lost in the large crowd that had gathered at the Albion.

"No Northenders!" complained Nimlet. "We've missed it."

Lucky said nothing; he could see the evidence of the raid. Groups of females were gathered around a couple of wounded males, and on the ground below the chestnut tree was a flurry of crows fighting over a . . . He shuddered. He didn't want to look.

The crowd let out a cheer as a Cloudfoot Patrol emerged

from the Northend trees. "They must have driven the raiders back," declared Nimlet. "It's not fair—we missed it."

Heading the troops was the finest squirrel Lucky had ever seen. "Is that the Patrol Leader?"

"Yes," said Nimlet reverently. "Isn't he great?"

Lucky nodded dumbly as the battered warrior went straight to comfort the fallen squirrel's mother. He then stopped to check on every wounded soldier, ignoring the cheering crowds. Finally, amid stamping feet and clapping paws, he went to receive thanks from Great Ma Cloudfoot.

Lucky had never seen her before, but he knew it was the Ma—she radiated authority from nose to tail-tip. Gesturing regally for silence, she addressed the crowd.

"Cloudfoots! Today we give thanks, once again, for the bravery and dedication of our Watch and Patrol. Sacrifices have been made, but the enemy has been repulsed and our Avenue is safe again. Victory is ours!"

The cheering crowds went wild as the Ma gathered together her Daughter Generals and left the trees.

"So, gentlemen," said a dry voice by their side. "Perhaps *now* you will take your training for the Watch and Patrol seriously."

Lucky and Nimlet nodded solemnly to the Trial Instructor. This wasn't a game—this was war.

11

Wrestling

Lucky arrived at First Daughter's drey at dusk, hardly able to drag himself along the branches. He'd been on Patrolling Exercises since dawn with Nimlet and he was exhausted. *It's okay for Nimlet*, thought Lucky. *Now he's fit, he never gets tired.*

He heard voices in the drey and stopped—*that sounded like the Ma!* He knew it was wrong, but he crept up to the entrance to listen.

"This is a very worrying development, Patrol Leader."

Lucky got closer—the Patrol Leader was in there?

"Yes, ma'am, it wasn't the usual rabble. They were organized. The Watch Squirrel on the first chestnut didn't stand a chance."

"Did they take much?" This was First Daughter's voice.

"Yes, ma'am—several batches of food. It's the biggest raiding party I've ever encountered." He paused, as if uncertain whether to say more. "I—I fear there was more than one Family."

"That's impossible," snapped the Ma. "Northenders never work together!"

Lucky jumped guiltily as someone pulled at his tail. "Lucky," whispered Mazie angrily. "What d'you think you're doing? Come away at once."

"The Patrol Leader's in there."

"Yes, and so is the Ma! It's no business of yours, Lucky—leave it to the Ma and the Daughter Generals."

"But the Patrol Leader said—"

"Forget what he said," she snapped. "You're just a cadet—you'll follow orders like every other male!"

They crept away from the drey and Mazie got a proper look at Lucky. *Tooth and claw*, she thought, *he looks worn out*. "Are you okay?"

"I can't keep up," said Lucky miserably. "It's fine at first, but then I get so tired. I *want* to keep up! Nimlet says we could join the Patrol Leader's troop when we've finished the Trials, and I really want to do that."

Mazie couldn't say what she was thinking: She wasn't

sure Lucky would even make the Final Run at this rate. "Is Nimlet helping you?" she asked instead.

"Oh, yes—but he's not great either. He's really strong now, you know, but he can't see very well and he misses the targets a lot."

Mazie had heard gossip of this already. Only a day or so ago, Nimlet had fallen through the trees and landed on a group of cadets. One of them was still in his drey recovering—his mother was furious.

"Surely the Patrolling Exercises are nearly over?" she questioned.

Lucky nodded.

"What's next?"

"Wrestling."

"Oh dear," said Mazie.

All the cadets were looking forward to Wrestling. At last they could do some real fighting!

The Trial Instructor had other ideas. "Gentlemen, this is not a free-for-all. There will be no scrapping or brawling in this troop. We are here to learn a skill."

The young males were disappointed—they'd been looking forward to some ruck and tumble.

"The skill of wrestling is one of defense," the Instructor continued. "We Cloudfoots, unlike the *rabble* Northenders, do not attack other clans. If an enemy attacks, we shall defend. If he will not surrender and retreat"—he paused for effect—"*then* we will Cast him Down!"

"With No Mercy!" chanted the males, stamping their feet.

"Indeed," said Ratter drily. "So, gentlemen, you will learn to fight like Cloudfoots. Let us begin on the training ground."

The troop scurried down to a clearing in the center of the Avenue that was surrounded by thick bushes. A Watch Squirrel had been posted to keep a close lookout for any incoming threat. Just to be on the safe side, the squirrels' friend, Mr. Finlay, was also quietly padding around the perimeter.

They started with crouches and maneuvering to find the best holds. There was a lot of good-natured jostling and shoving as squirrels tumbled among the dead leaves.

Lucky was paired with the witty squirrel, of "call me 'rat'" fame, and they ducked and dove around each other, trying to grab at fur. Lucky was quick, and easily dodged his opponent. This wasn't as bad as he had thought it was going to be!

"Enough," cried Ratter. The cadets must have let off

enough steam by now. It was time to get down to some serious training. "Mr. Nimlet, come here, please."

Nimlet advanced warily.

"Don't look so concerned, Mr. Nimlet, this is just a demonstration."

The other squirrels laughed—*they* weren't the ones being demonstrated on.

"Any attacker on a branch will instinctively drop to his hindquarters . . ." said Ratter. Nimlet dropped. "And raise his forearms to strike." Nimlet raised his forearms. "This leaves him vulnerable, gentlemen, to the classic wrestling hold of the armlock."

Ratter grabbed Nimlet's arm, twisted it up behind his back, and tried to complete the lock. Normally, the unfortunate cadet would fall to his knees begging for release. Nimlet's rock-solid arm didn't move. *Bud and branch! That's no longer fat, it's muscle!* thought Ratter. He hastily dropped Nimlet's arm to cover his surprise. "Your turn, gentlemen, to practice this hold."

The witty squirrel held up his arms and Lucky grabbed and twisted the nearest limb, but he was flung easily to the ground before he could finish the hold. He jumped up and tried again. Again he was floored.

"Change."

"I'll try not to hurt you," said the witty squirrel.

"Thanks," muttered Lucky.

It really, really hurt.

He limped home at the end of the day with Nimlet at his side. He'd been thrown, spun, sat on, and clinched. Every bone in his body ached. Nimlet, on the other hand, had thrown, spun, sat on, and successfully clinched every squirrel he'd been paired with. He was a natural.

"I'm looking forward to tomorrow. Ratter's promised to show us the tail-throw!" he said enthusiastically.

"Right," said Lucky weakly.

"Then we're going to move back up to the training branches."

"Can't wait," muttered Lucky.

"Then we'll have the proper Wrestling Trial, in front of the Ma *and* the Patrol Leader!"

What? No one had mentioned this to Lucky! "D'you mean in front of *everyone*?"

"Oh, yes," said Nimlet happily. "It's a proper wrestling match. The whole Clan will be there."

"Oh, that's great! The whole Clan. There. To see me fail."

"I'm not going to let you fail! We'll practice together. I'll help you."

"I don't think that's going to work, Nim."

"Don't worry! We'll both be wrestling champions!" He slapped him on the back and Lucky yelped with pain. "Oh—sorry."

12

Ratter

Lucky faced his opponent on the branch and concentrated hard. Watch him carefully, Nimlet had said. Anticipate his moves. The squirrel leapt toward him and Lucky dodged left as his opponent made a clumsy grab to the right. Lucky spun around, pounced on his back, and the squirrel fell flat on the branch. It worked! The squirrel raised himself up, but he seemed dazed and Lucky easily tackled him again. *I'm winning!* thought Lucky.

"Cadet!" called Ratter, shaking his head. "You will wrestle Mr. Lucky correctly." The youngster looked guiltily at his feet and Lucky felt a hot rush of anger and shame. *He let me win!*

They came together again. This time he was thrown effortlessly down and clinched. Before Ratter could say anything, Lucky fled the training branches, furiously fighting back tears. He hated wrestling!

The cadets all shuffled uncomfortably as they watched him go. They didn't want to fight Lucky—there was no glory to be won there. Nimlet was a different matter: He'd wrestled down every squirrel in the troop—he was unstoppable!

Ratter had even drafted in two ex-cadets, who'd already joined the Watch and Patrol, to teach Nimlet a lesson. His troop-mates watched with a mixture of admiration and envy as he beat them too.

Nimlet should have been triumphant and happy, but he was too worried about Lucky . . . and so was Ratter.

Mazie Trimble formally announced the Trial Instructor into First Daughter's drey and she greeted him warmly. "I do not often get the pleasure of your company, old friend. Your cadets keep you very busy."

"Indeed, ma'am, and one has been keeping me busier than most."

Ah, thought First Daughter, *of course. He's come to see me about Lucky.* "I heard that you have generously been giving my son extra training."

"Yes, ma'am, and Mr. Nimlet has been helping him too."

"Nimlet the unbeaten wrestling champion. Second Daughter must be very pleased."

Your spiteful sister shows more interest in Lucky's failure, thought the Instructor, but he kept this to himself.

"Ma'am, I will get to the point, painful as it is. Lucky cannot possibly take part in the Wrestling Trial. Truly, I have done all I can. I have *never* had a cadet fail the Final Run—I cannot have this happen now. Your son must withdraw."

First Daughter's eyes narrowed. If Lucky withdrew now she might as well Cast him Down, and banish him from the Avenue today. "Lucky will wrestle, Trial Instructor," she said coldly.

"He will be publicly defeated, ma'am—and humiliated."

"Then make it as quick and painless as possible," ordered First Daughter. *I am going to lose my son*, she thought, *and there's nothing else I can do to save him.*

That afternoon, a very nervous Nimlet was summoned to Ratter's drey. It was in one of the oldest and most

85

spectacular chestnut trees in the Avenue, and it was also next to the Albion gates and the Northend border. The Trial Instructor liked to keep a close eye on the enemy.

Nimlet shuffled unhappily from foot to foot and his bushy tail twitched with a life of its own. *Why does Ratter want to see me? I bet it won't be good news.* The interview, however, started off rather well.

"Mr. Nimlet, I had low expectations when you first joined the Cadet Troop, but you have proved me wrong."

"I have?" This was a surprise—Ratter admitting he was wrong!

"Indeed. All students in Wrestling lose at least one bout. But you have beaten every opponent paws down, apart from me, of course."

"You want *us* to wrestle?" Nimlet couldn't hide his horror.

"Tooth and claw—no!" Ratter shook his grizzly head, making a strange snorting sound. It was his attempt at laughter. It wasn't very good. "Mr. Nimlet, you have received the highest marks in Wrestling that I have ever given any student." Nimlet found himself glowing with pride. "I now need to consider very carefully who you are to be paired with for the Wrestling Trial."

A small niggle of doubt formed in Nimlet's mind.

"The opponents for the Wrestling Trial have been drawn

up," the Trial Instructor went on crisply, "and you will be paired with Mr. Lucky."

"But that's not fair!" exclaimed Nimlet, before he could stop himself.

"Of course it's not *fair*, Mr. Nimlet. But that's not the point. You have beaten every squirrel in your troop *and* two former cadets. You are the best wrestler of your year. Even the Patrol Leader has noticed you. You should be proud."

"Yes, but—it's just not fair!" spluttered Nimlet, close to tears, his tail swishing in distress.

Ratter sighed. "No, but it is logical. I will pair the cadets with equal abilities; it will be a fair contest for them. Mr. Lucky is going to fail the Wrestling Trial, whoever I pair him with, and you are going to pass."

"But Lucky is my friend!" wailed Nimlet.

"I am aware of that," snapped Ratter. "So you can make sure he is pinned with minimum harm and we can have a quick-surrender result. This is the best outcome for everyone concerned. Do I make myself clear?" He raised an inquiring eyebrow. What could Nimlet say? You didn't argue with the Trial Instructor. "Do I make myself clear, Mr. Nimlet?" Ratter repeated sharply.

Nimlet gave in and, nodding in dumb, miserable agreement, left the drey.

Lucky searched the trees for Nimlet—he hadn't seen him for days. At first Lucky had been lying low, too ashamed and embarrassed at running away from the training branches. But then he started to get worried. Was Nimlet angry with him? *I suppose Cloudfoots never run away*, he thought bitterly. He'd find him today. Ratter was announcing the pairings for the Wrestling Trial, so Nimlet had to be there.

Lucky joined the excited jostling cadets, waiting for Ratter to appear. There was Nimlet on another branch. *He won't even* look *at me*, thought Lucky. *What's going on?*

The Trial Instructor arrived and began to announce the pairings to the expectant gathering. It was too late for Lucky to talk to his friend.

Ratter went down the list. "And finally," he said, "Mr. Nimlet will wrestle with Mr. Lucky."

There was a gasp of horror from the cadets. That wasn't fair! Lucky took one look at Nimlet's guilty face and guessed that he already knew. No wonder Nimlet had been avoiding him!

It never occurred to him that Nimlet was supposed to beat him. He could only think of one reason for the pairing. Quivering with rage, he scurried over to the branch.

"I don't care what Ratter's told you to do. You're going to fight me properly—you *stinking* Cloudfoot!" Nimlet tried to interrupt, but Lucky was too furious to listen. "He can't bear to lose face, can he? He trained me and I'm going to fail. So that . . . that *rat* has told you to let me win—I can't believe you'd do that, Nimlet!"

"Lucky, that's not it—you've got it all wr—"

"Shut up!" screamed Lucky. "You'd better fight me fair, Nimlet—because it's no surrender! I'm going to fight you to . . . to . . . to a pulp!" And he leapt off the branch and sped into the distance.

Nimlet sat dazed and confused. This was all horribly wrong. He wished he had someone to talk to, but the only real friend he'd ever had was Lucky.

And, after the Wrestling Trial, Nimlet knew that Lucky would never talk to him again.

13

Trial

The big day was drawing closer and the Avenue was alive with tumbling, chattering males getting more and more excited. All the cadets were frantically practicing their wrestling skills—except for Nimlet, who spent the days alone, wandering unhappily from tree to tree. Lucky wouldn't come anywhere near him and he had no idea what to do.

Disobeying Ratter was unthinkable; none of the other cadets could help him and Mazie would just tell him to follow orders.

What would happen afterward? If Lucky surrendered, then he would be banished from the Cloudfoot trees. *I'll never see him again*, Nimlet thought wretchedly. *I don't*

want to join the Patrol Leader's troop, not without Lucky—
there's got to be something *I can do!*

But try as he might, there didn't seem to be any way out, and on the morning of the Wrestling Trial he had to join the other cadets in the arena. There was Lucky, scowling angrily, and Nimlet knew it was too late to explain.

The Trial site was between two old sycamore trees that grew closely together. The cadets could wrestle in the mesh of branches not too far from Ground-level, so any thrown squirrel would land safely on a soft bed of leaves.

There was a good turnout; every Cloudfoot wanted to see the cadets wrestle. The trees still needed defending, so messenger squirrels were ready to run the length of the Avenue with news. Every male in the Watch and Patrol had a son, brother, or cousin competing in the Trial, and if their family did well they wanted to know about it immediately!

The females gathered in groups exchanging the latest gossip. Old males were found comfortable viewing branches, but the best viewing place was set aside for Ma Cloudfoot and her First and Second Daughters. A special store of acorns, reserved for the occasion, was broken out and distributed among the crowd.

The gossiping and chatter stopped dead as the Trial Instructor entered the site. The spectators settled down for the traditional opening address. It began.

"Fellow Cloudfoots," announced the Instructor, "we are gathered here today to witness the strength, speed, and stamina of a new generation of males! We males learn the skill of wrestling to defend our Clan and our Avenue." The crowd murmured approval. "Our aim is not the Falling—"

"Quite right!" interrupted an old gray male before he was hushed.

"Our aim is for the enemy to surrender and retreat. If our enemy will not surrender, *then* he shall be Cast Down!"

"With No Mercy!" chanted the crowd.

"All holds are allowed, but the drawing of blood is not. A throw is a worthy outcome for both opponents, but surrender will result in banishment." All the Cloudfoot squirrels nodded; everyone understood this. "Let the Trial commence!"

The first wrestling pair came into the arena. First they bobbed to Ma Cloudfoot, who acknowledged their greeting with a formal nod. Then they scurried to the starting point and the Trial Instructor stood between them, holding back each at arm's length.

"Gentlemen," said Ratter crisply. "You may wrestle—now!" He jumped swiftly off the branch, and the two squirrels crashed together.

The cadets leaned forward to get a good view. Nimlet was keen to watch, despite himself. He'd wrestled both these large, strong males and they'd been tough opponents—which one would win here?

The two squirrels grappled, rolled, and twisted through the branches trying to get a hold. Finally they both tail-locked onto a branch and hung upside down, wrestling in midair.

That's great wrestling, thought Nimlet, impressed.

The audience was enthralled, and even Ratter had a small smile of approval on his face. The males seemed evenly balanced in speed and skill, but the contest wore down their strength, and the inevitable happened. One squirrel was unbalanced and thrown. He crashed down through the branches, twisting and spinning, trying to get a hold. But he was falling too fast and plunged toward the ground. The crowd groaned.

He hit Ground-level with a heavy *thud*—but immediately jumped up and accepted defeat with a gracious tail gesture. The crowd went wild with delight. What a show of sportsmanship!

The next pair of contestants were twin brothers, and everyone waited with eager anticipation. Rivals from birth, they had begged Ratter to pair them. This was going to be a serious fight.

The squirrels came together like deadly enemies, grim-faced, with no holds barred. Neither could get a firm hold—they had an uncanny ability to judge each other's moves. Up and down the branches, frantically trying to find a weakness, the two furious brothers wrestled on and on.

At first the crowd shouted their encouragement. But cheers turned to groans as the two males became increasingly battered and exhausted, and eventually Ratter slid between them and pushed them apart. They strained to continue, glaring at each other, gasping for breath, their tails thrashing and shaking wildly.

"Gentlemen, please!" said Ratter, still having to hold them apart. "I'm afraid we don't have all day." The delighted audience tittered. "We shall resort to the tiebreaker."

The brothers, taken to two opposite trees, scurried out to the end of the branches that almost touched. Whichever squirrel could grapple and throw his opponent off first would win.

But it was the usual tiebreaker result. Neither squirrel, wrestling on the slender branch tips, could keep their balance. They both fell, unbelievably still grappling, dropping swiftly through the air. There was a stunned silence as the brothers hit the ground, still locked grimly together.

It was an honorable draw, and everyone should be happy—that was the theory. The males stood up shaking off the dead leaves; they turned to face each other, battered and spent, and you could have heard a nut drop in the surrounding trees. The audience held its breath.

Suddenly they were embracing each other, grinning widely from ear to ear, and the crowd let out a sigh of relief. The cheers and stomping of feet were deafening as the twins slapped each other on the back and held their paws up together in a victory salute. No one would have believed that they had been fighting like mortal enemies moments before. Waving to their family (their mother was in tears), they staggered off, exhausted, arm in arm, to be congratulated by the other cadets.

Now it was time for Lucky and Nimlet.

14

Enemies

Ratter wanted to get Lucky and Nimlet's bout over with as early as possible. They made a ridiculous pair, standing on either side of him on the starting branch.

The crowd was not impressed, and there was a low rumble of discontent; mutterings of "no contest" and "not fair" could be heard running through the trees. This was going to be a very short bout.

Second Daughter sat on the viewing branch next to the Ma, trying not to let her emotions show. She was greedily anticipating the downfall of her hated sister's weakling son.

First Daughter sat stony-faced. She dared not glance in Mazie's direction. The young female knew nothing of wrestling, but she'd been missing from the drey for days. *Trying to help him*, thought First Daughter. *But it's too late now.*

The Trial Instructor held them at arm's length. The spectators settled down, waiting for the inevitable to happen quickly. "Gentlemen, you may wrestle—now!"

Ratter skipped backward off the branch and Nimlet lunged with all his strength. *I'll pin him down fast and get it over with*, he thought. But instead, Nimlet found himself flat on the branch, clutching at thin air. Where had Lucky gone?

Now he dropped down onto Nimlet's head and bounced quickly off, leaving Nimlet dazed and hurt. What was Lucky doing?

Lucky glared down from the next tree, tail swishing violently. "Come on, Cloudfoot!" he jeered. "What're you waiting for?"

Nimlet lunged again, but Lucky was too fast and tricky. Somersaulting backward off the branch, he dove swiftly down and, after a stunning head kick, he sprang off, out of reach again. The audience gasped in horror. What sort of wrestling was this?

With watering eyes and ringing ears, Nimlet rose angrily from the branch while Lucky leapt around the tree above him.

"Come here and fight like a Cloudfoot!" Nimlet shouted.

A red blur swung down from the tree and Nimlet leapt up and grasped at Lucky's feet; at last he had him—and he wasn't going to let go!

Locked together, they rolled and tumbled down the tree until Nimlet managed to lash his tail to a branch and stop the fall. The crowd cheered and frantically signaled approval—this was more like it!

Still in the high branches, Ratter couldn't see what was happening. *This needs to end quickly*, he thought.

"Right!" panted Nimlet, pinning Lucky down. "We are going to fight by the rules, and *you* are going to surrender." Lucky struggled under the squirrel's weight, his hind legs kicking, desperate to break free. "Surrender now!" demanded Nimlet.

"I—don't—think—so," Lucky gasped. Twisting around, with all his strength he bit into Nimlet's arm.

Surprise and searing pain loosened Nimlet's grip and Lucky half wriggled out—but Nimlet grabbed Lucky's neck. Through a haze of pain and fury he held on with all his might. No escape this time!

"Surrender, you runt!" he spat. "Surrender or I'll Cast you Down!"

"Never," Lucky croaked.

"Surrender, you fool!" shrieked Nimlet, tightening his grip.

"No." It was a whisper.

Lucky went limp as he passed out. "Surrender!" Nimlet screamed, shaking Lucky furiously.

"Mr. Nimlet!" The Trial Instructor's stern voice cut in from the branches far above. "Mr. Nimlet, I must point out that your opponent cannot surrender if he is unconscious."

Nimlet looked down in horror at his friend. *What am I doing? This can't be real—how could I have done this?* Lucky slid slowly down and slumped at his feet, and Nimlet sobbed as he leaned over the lifeless squirrel.

"Lucky! Lucky, please wake up," he begged. "I wasn't supposed to let you win—it wasn't like that! I was supposed to beat you quickly—I didn't want to hurt you!" Tears ran down his face and blood trickled down his arm.

He started to shake the squirrel, desperate for him to move, and Lucky finally coughed and shuddered into life. Nimlet picked him up, thumping him on the back as Lucky fought for air.

"E-e-enough, Nimlet," he managed to gasp.

They sat on the branch, hanging tightly to each other, Lucky still taking great gulps of air.

"I am so sorry, Lucky. Ratter said it was the right thing to do. Please surrender."

"Ratter wanted you to beat me?" he croaked, finally understanding.

Nimlet nodded miserably. "I should never have agreed. I knew it wasn't fair—I'm so sorry." He started sobbing again.

"Throw me down, Nim," whispered Lucky hoarsely.

"What?"

"It's the only way. I'll never be accepted as a Cloudfoot, but I won't surrender. So throw me down."

Nimlet's world snapped into sharp focus. With a wonderful cool certainty he knew just what to do. That it was the *right* thing to do. He clasped Lucky closely with his good arm and leapt off the branch, Casting them both Down into the cold winter's air. The loud *thud* as the two squirrels hit the ground echoed through the trees, and the crowd was deathly silent. What had happened?

Ratter knew—he was going to have to declare a draw. He was furious! Lucky could take part in the Final Run now.

He spiraled down the sycamore trunk to Ground-level, not daring to look at First Daughter. "Mr. Lucky—" he began, then stopped, seeing Nimlet's bloody arm. Ah! Now he could disqualify Lucky! "There seems to be some irregularity here," he said coldly, masking his relief. "There is a blood wound on your arm, Mr. Nimlet. You have been bitten."

Nimlet glanced down at his arm. "Oh, no, sir," he lied smoothly. "I'm so clumsy I scratched it on a branch." He looked the old squirrel squarely in the eye, daring him to disagree. "So you'll be declaring a draw," said Nimlet. It was a statement, not a question.

Ratter was so angry that he was lost for words. He had been wrong, very wrong—*neither* of these squirrels was Cloudfoot material.

15

The Plan

"Ouch!" Nimlet tried to pull away from Mazie's firm grip. "Miss Trimble, you're hurting me!"

"Don't you 'Miss Trimble' me, you stupid male. If I don't clean it properly, that arm really will hurt."

"But, Mazie, don't you think it's clean—"

She spun toward Lucky. "And you! What did you think *you* were doing? Cloudfoots don't bite when they wrestle. I never told you to bite him, did I?"

"No, Mazie," said Lucky, hanging his head.

"Avoid him, that's what I said. In and out quickly—don't let him get a hold," she carried on crossly, licking the wound clean. "There, that's the best I can do. Now come along, we're leaving."

Nimlet looked confused. "Where are we going?"

"To a quiet and secluded drey I know. First Daughter wants you both out of the way. Nimlet needs to recover and the gossip needs to die down. You've caused her enough trouble as it is."

Lucky and Nimlet followed Mazie unhappily out into the trees. They saw groups of squirrels on other branches who all scurried quickly away as they approached. Lucky spotted the witty squirrel with some other cadets and signaled a greeting, but the males turned their backs. No one wanted to talk to them.

Lucky was puzzled. "Why are they all avoiding us?"

Mazie sighed. "They don't understand what happened at the Trial, but they know you didn't act like Cloudfoots. They don't want you in the Clan."

"But that's not fair," said Lucky. "I know *I'm* not a Cloudfoot—but Nimlet is!"

"I don't want to be a Cloudfoot," declared Nimlet, "if it means following orders you know aren't right!"

Lucky was horrified. "Nim, I don't even *look* like a Cloudfoot. How was I ever going to fit in? But you—you're a wrestling champion! You can easily do the Final Run—join the Patrol Leader's—"

"Forget that!" interrupted Nimlet. "I've tried 'fitting in' and I'm not joining the Patrol Leader's troop without you. We're in this together."

Lucky shut up.

They traveled a long way south, down a strangely deserted Avenue. The chestnuts had given way to beech and oak. Finally they came to a gaunt old ash tree where a sagging and poorly made drey hung in the branches. Inside, Nimlet looked around in disgust at the carpet of moldy leaves and the leaking roof.

"Who lives in a dump like this?" he asked.

"My family," said Mazie shortly. "Stay here, I'm going out to forage."

"I didn't know!" said Nimlet, as she left the drey in a huff. "I didn't mean to make her cross."

"It doesn't take much, Nim. Maybe if we cleaned it up a bit?"

When Mazie got back with the food, the drey had been swept clean and the males had, rather clumsily, rewoven the worst holes in the walls. They shared the food in silence. Was she ever going to talk to them again?

Mazie finished her grooming and decided she'd punished them enough. "So, cadets, tell me about this Final Run."

"Don't you know?" asked Nimlet, surprised.

"Strangely enough, *Mr.* Nimlet, we females concentrate on learning the Knowledge. I know you have to do a run—but I don't know what it entails."

At least she still wants to talk to me, thought Nimlet, and he started to explain. "It starts at dawn, down by the Good Shepherd."

"Near the gates at the south end of the Avenue?"

"Yes," said Nimlet. "And ends at the Albion."

"The Good Shepherd to the Albion," said Mazie, frowning. "That's the whole Avenue!" How would Lucky manage that?

"Oh, the run's not a problem," said Nimlet. "The problem's the Watch and Patrol out to hunt us."

"What?!"

"There're six Watch Squirrels stationed along the run, and random Patrols. You have to either sneak past them or outrun them."

Tooth and claw! thought Mazie. *Outrun them? Lucky can't outrun anything!*

"If they catch you," continued Nimlet, "you can wrestle— you just have to get past them all and reach the Albion by sunset."

"I see," said Mazie, frantically calculating the run-time. It was close to true No-Growth, the nights long and the days short. How could they possibly do this together? "I have an idea," she said. "Nimlet, you can out-wrestle any squirrel. If you're spotted, you could take care of the Watch and Patrol, while Lucky sneaks past."

"That's a good plan!" said Nimlet.

"No, it's not," said Lucky hotly. "I'm not having you do my fighting for me! What sort of a scrub d'you take me for?"

"Lucky, don't be angry—we're only trying to help," said Mazie.

Lucky opened his mouth to say more, but seeing the look on his friends' faces, he stopped. "Oh, feed-me-to-foxes, I'm sorry. I know you're trying to help. Don't worry; we'll think of something, I know we will."

I can't think of another plan, thought Mazie, *but I can help them practice.*

The next morning they set to work. Mazie came up with a training program, and she began by taking the role of the Watch while the two males tried to sneak past her. At first she spotted them easily and insisted they try again and again; she was very strict.

"She's worse than Ratter!" complained Nimlet.

But slowly they got better. Nimlet still missed his aim sometimes, and crashed clumsily through the trees, so Lucky suggested he learned to dive off the branches on purpose— it got you down a tree in record speed and was a great way to escape the Patrol. The pair of squirrels spent many hours spiraling up to the Canopy, then dive-bombing through the branches and swinging to safety at the very last minute.

Any other cadets seeing this would think they'd gone crazy. A missed paw-hold could mean a fatal fall, and constantly being up that high was just asking to get taken by a bird. Most of the cadets avoided the Canopy if they could and left the Ground-level to the foraging females—they stuck to the safe Mid-levels. This gave Lucky an idea, and he began to formulate a plan.

When he told Mazie, she was impressed by the daring and logic. It was a very well-thought-out plan for a male. But she didn't like it much, and Nimlet was dead against the idea.

"It's insane, Lucky. We can't run down the whole of the Avenue on top of the Canopy! Going that high, even for the short time we do, is dangerous enough!"

"But there'll be no Watch and Patrol up there," argued Lucky. "No one's going to spot us so high up, Nim. We'll have a clear run."

"No one? No one but the odd hungry crow or ravenous raven! Why d'you think the Canopy's a squirrel-free zone?"

"Yes, it's a squirrel-free zone, that's why it's so perfect. Look, here's an idea. What if we start off in the Canopy and go as far as we can? Then if we spot anything that might be dangerous—"

"Well, that's everything up there," muttered Nimlet.

"Anything that might be dangerous," continued Lucky, ignoring him, "*then* we'll drop down to the Mid-levels. We could even drop farther!"

"Oh, that's a great idea," said Nimlet sarcastically. "Let's do the rest of the Run at Ground-level. So if the birds don't get us, the foxes will!"

"No one's going to get us." Lucky patted his friend cheerfully on the back. "I'll look out for you—and you can flatten anything that gets in our way. It's a perfect plan!"

It's a crazy plan, thought Nimlet, *but it might work*. No squirrel in the Watch and Patrol would think of taking the route, so it *would* be a clear run.

A clear and dangerous run.

16

Taken

Tarragon was very worried that her uncle wasn't going to forgive her. He'd ordered her to stay in the drey and she'd been cooped up for days and days. It was so . . . dreary!

She was bored silly and missed her old companion. Juniper, the new one, was no fun at all; she didn't even know any jokes or games! They even had to do lessons. Stupid stuff like history, which was all about old battles. Useless!

But she didn't dare complain to her uncle, because he'd been terribly angry when he'd found her with the fox. She often remembered the fox. The little vixen cub had been *so* pretty—she had the best tail Tarragon had ever seen. *I wish*

I had a tail like that, she thought. *And I'm sure we could have been friends—she wasn't* really *hunting me. I think Mr. Finlay's there to protect me too—like my uncle.*

Tarragon's uncle had been very busy. The Cloudfoot raid with his Coppice allies had gone well. His troops had tasted blood. Fleet and Coppice squirrels had feasted on Cloudfoot food. News of the success had spread through the Northend. Several other Families had shown interest in joining his alliance.

What he needed now was something to stir them all into action, something they could all unite over. Something . . . or some*one.*

After what seemed like endless dull days, to Tarragon's immense relief, the Major finally came to call.

"Ooh-ooh, Uncle, I'm so pleased to see you—you haven't come for ages!"

"Important Family affairs have kept me very busy," said the Major, smiling. "So, how are you today, my dear?"

"Uncle, I'm *so* bored stuck in this stuffy drey."

"Well, my dear, you shouldn't have disobeyed me because—"

"You know best!" interrupted Tarragon brightly.

"Yes, I do. So have you learned your lesson? Will you obey me now?"

Tarragon nodded. "I promise, Uncle, I promise to obey you at all times." She gave him her best wide-eyed smile. "So can I go out now?"

Major Fleet patted her on the head. "You'd like a little outing?"

"Ooh-ooh, yes, please!"

"Very well. Ready yourself, and I shall go and have words with Juniper."

Tarragon couldn't wait; it had been so long since she'd seen the trees. But when she poked her nose out of the drey her whiskers stiffened in shock. "Uncle, the trees are bare! Where have all the leaves gone?"

"This is the time of No-Growth. The leaves will come back at Bud-time."

"Are you sure?" asked Tarragon doubtfully. "They don't look like they'll ever have leaves again."

The Major laughed. "Sometimes I forget how very young you are, niece." *But not*, he thought, *how foolish*. "Come, I want to introduce you to my ally, Major Coppice. Then we will visit the Families Bracken and Glade."

"Ooh-ooh, goody!" Tarragon clapped her paws in delight. Visiting! She'd never done that before.

The common squirrels waved and cheered loudly as the Honorable Mistress passed by. What a relief! They'd not seen her for many days, and it had been worrying.

"Greet your Family, Tarragon," said the Major. "You are well-loved in our trees."

"Yes, I am, aren't I!" she said happily. "It's so nice!"

The Major gritted his teeth. This was going to be a long day.

For Tarragon the day could have lasted forever, she was having so much fun. She met lots of new Families and they were all delighted to see her. It was wonderful. They had just finished visiting in the trees near the Albion when she spotted her companion rushing toward them. Tarragon's heart sank. *Oh no! She's come to take me home. She's going to spoil everything!*

"Stay here, my dear. I'll go and see what she wants," said the Major, and he scurried off to meet the female.

Tarragon could see his face darken and his tail signal anger as Juniper chattered at him. They raced back toward her. "Tarragon, I want you to go with your companion immediately. Get out of the way quickly. Hide up in the Canopy. We are being attacked."

"What?"

"There's a Cloudfoot raiding party at the Albion gates, and I have to warn the Families. I should never have brought you down here."

Tarragon hesitated; she'd never been up high in the trees before.

"Go—both of you. As high up as you can!" snapped the Major. "That's an order!" And, turning tail, he sped off back through the Mid-levels.

"Come on," said Juniper, and she started to spiral up the tree.

The trees near the Albion were the tallest in the Northend. They climbed and climbed, with Juniper showing no signs of stopping. The higher they went, the more frightened Tarragon began to feel. *But I've promised to follow orders*, she thought, *and Honorable females aren't frightened of anything!* She ground her teeth in determination and climbed steadily higher.

It became lighter as the branches began to thin out. She couldn't see Juniper now, and the glare of the sunlight was blinding in the clear winter sky. *Ooh-ooh, I don't like this*, she thought. *It's not nice.*

A vast expanse of blue glowered above and Tarragon had to stop. She sank her claws rigidly into the bark, feeling terribly sick and dizzy. Black spots floated before her eyes. She shook her head and blinked rapidly and her vision cleared—but Juniper was still nowhere to be seen.

Tarragon forced herself to claw up to the end of the topmost branch and she desperately scanned the bare black branches of the Canopy. *It's no good—I can't see her. Where has she gone?* The treetops swayed dangerously in the air currents and she clung, terrified, to the rocking branch.

Ooh-ooh, I feel sick, I'm going to be sick. I want to go home! The black spots were dancing before her eyes again. *I'm going to faint! I'm going to faint and fall!* She shook her head, desperate to see, but the spots still reeled. *No!* Tarragon's eyes widened in raw fear.

Tooth and whisker—not spots! It was one circling black-and-white shape, getting bigger and bigger . . . and bigger . . . Too late she let out a squeal of terror—cut horribly short as the shape swooped down. A cloak of rattling feathers engulfed her and the whole sky blacked out.

Claws closed around her neck. Breathless, she plunged into a well of deep, terrifying darkness.

Tarragon was lifted, unconscious, from the Canopy. She didn't see Juniper watching from below, smiling. The massive magpie swooped away, carrying the lifeless form dangling from its claws.

This has all worked out rather nicely, Juniper thought.

17

The Final Run

Miss Trimble, you achieved the highest grade for Strategy in your year, did you not?" inquired First Daughter.

"Yes, ma'am."

"So what do you think? Do you really believe that Lucky's plan will work?"

Mazie hesitated. "It's dangerous, ma'am, but I think it's their only option."

First Daughter nodded. "Very well; send in the Trial Instructor and I shall play my part."

"Ma'am," said Ratter, bobbing as he entered the drey. He hoped very much that she wasn't going to make some unreasonable demand.

"Old friend, I have a request."

Ratter sighed; he knew it would be a favor.

"I know we don't have much time. The Final Run commences at dawn and I have come to a decision."

Ratter brightened. Had she come to her senses at last? Was she going to withdraw Lucky from the Run?

"I realize that I was wrong. I should have listened to your wise advice and withdrawn Lucky from the Wrestling Trial. He will, of course, fail the Run, and I am truly sorry that this will spoil your faultless reputation. But I cannot withdraw him now."

The Instructor tried to hide his look of disappointment.

"However," she continued briskly, "I have a plan you might approve of. I would like you to send Lucky and Nimlet out first. Alone. Give them a head start."

"But, ma'am—"

"Let me finish. I know it is customary to start with the best cadets, but if you station a Patrol in all of the first ash trees, Lucky can be intercepted and eliminated immediately. He need not be seen in the Avenue again."

"I see," said Ratter. He was very impressed—she was more ruthless than he had thought! "But what about Mr. Nimlet?"

"I have no interest in my sister's son," First Daughter said coldly. "Though I suggest you station your best wrestlers along the Avenue, if you wish him to be eliminated too."

"Of course!" The old squirrel bobbed happily. "Indeed, ma'am, I shall do exactly as you request." *She will make a great Ma, when the time comes*, he thought as he left the drey.

There was no ceremony or crowd on Cloudfoot Avenue the morning of the Final Run. The Daughters stayed quietly in their dreys, along with the old males, keeping well out of the way. This was Watch and Patrol business.

The cadets gathered at the Good Shepherd gates as dawn was breaking, and the Trial Instructor split them into running order. There was no comment or surprise shown when Lucky and Nimlet were named as the first to go—the cadets realized that Cloudfoot rules applied to them, but not to Lucky and Nimlet. They didn't care. Lucky and Nimlet had no friends that morning.

The signal was given.

Lucky turned to Nimlet and grasped his arm. "Good-speed?"

Nimlet grinned and nodded in agreement. "Good-speed!" And they both bounded off into the Mid-levels, heading north up the Avenue.

Ratter watched them go with a look of grim satisfaction

on his face. The Watch and Patrol had been briefed to show no mercy.

The two squirrels darted along the Mid-level branches until they were well out of sight of the Good Shepherd gates. Then they both began to claw up a tree trunk, rapidly and silently. The success of their plan depended upon no one seeing them going up into the Canopy.

Nimlet climbed behind Lucky with grim concentration. If he was clumsy and noisy now it would ruin everything. Lucky reached the highest branches and scouted for incoming. He signaled the all-clear and they began to work their way along the Canopy.

They soon reached the group of ash trees and Lucky pointed to the branches far below—there, as expected, was the Patrol waiting to catch them.

Nimlet squinted. "I can't see them," he complained.

"Shush!" whispered Lucky. "I can—but they won't look up here as long as we're quiet."

They crept along the branches, freezing at every creaking twig and spar. *This is taking too long*, thought Lucky, but he didn't dare go any faster.

They had just gotten to the last ash tree when two crows launched themselves out of the treetops ahead. "Incoming!" Lucky screamed before he could stop himself, and the squirrels leapt down to the branches below.

"Psst!" An old gray head peeped from a nook in the tree trunk. "In here, lads—quick!"

Lucky and Nimlet didn't need to be told twice, and scurried into the old male's home.

"Stay here," the squirrel ordered, and he went out onto his branch. The squirrels now saw him waving to the Patrol below. "Didn't get me!" he shouted. "Don't need assistance, you lads just carry on, eh?" He came back to the hidey-hole in the trunk, rubbing his paws together briskly. "That should do it. Don't think they spotted you, so give them a minute and you can get on, eh?"

"Th-thank you—" spluttered Nimlet.

"Pah! No need. Bit of a risk, though, lads, doing the Final Run in the Canopy. You're a plucky pair!"

"Please don't tell!" said Lucky.

"Tell? Tell who? It's a good plan if you don't meet the birds. Takes me back to my Final Run—I wasn't always this old, you know." He laughed wheezily and, rubbing his paws, again stuck his nose out of the hole in the trunk. "Right, lads, I reckon it's all clear, but you need to crack on if you're going to get to the Albion by sunset."

The squirrels got beyond the ash trees and picked up the pace. It was hard going. The treetops swayed in the air currents, making balance difficult, and they often had to double back to find close enough branches to leap onto.

Then there was incoming. Twice they had to spiral down a trunk to avoid hunting birds. The third time was a false alarm—the dark shape turned out to be a lone greylag goose, honking morosely for its lost mate.

"I thought you were good at spotting birds," grumbled Nimlet.

"How was I to know it was a goose!" said Lucky. He was getting tired.

"I want a turn as lookout," said Nimlet.

"You? You're as blind as a bat!"

"Yeah? Well, you're as slow as a worm!"

They had only gone a third of the way along the Avenue, and the sun had reached its highest point in the sky. Lucky was starting to slow down.

"We should stop for a bit," suggested Nimlet.

"I don't think so. We'll never reach the Albion by sunset if we don't keep going," Lucky answered. But he did stop for a few moments and clung to a branch, taking long deep breaths.

"You won't get to the Albion at all if you don't have a rest," said Nimlet, who wasn't a bit tired. "I might be able to keep going, but I need you as lookout. I'm as blind as a bat, remember? I mean, what's that? That flappy dark thing over there?" He gestured toward the Albion.

"Oh, I expect it's another goose," said Lucky dully, rousing himself to look. *That's a strange shape*, he thought, though it was difficult to focus through the glare of sunlight. He narrowed his eyes and a chill ran down his spine. Nimlet sensed him stiffen.

"What is it?"

"Magpie," said Lucky shortly.

"Forget that! Even I can tell that's not a magpie shape."

"It's a magpie shape when it's got a squirrel hanging from its claws," said Lucky grimly.

18

Rescue

The limp body of the squirrel was a dead weight in the magpie's grip, dragging him down toward the treetops. He was nearly back to his own airspace, but . . . why not lighten the load?

"Cack!" *Take the eyes and liver?* "Cack!" *A snack! A snack!* "Cack! Cack!" The bird descended into the Canopy, intent on his meal.

The attack came out of nowhere. A gray-furred shape hurled painfully into his side. *What? What?* "Cack! Cack!" His hold loosened on the squirrel and she dropped like a stone through the branches.

Mine! "Cack!" He bowed to swoop after the meat, but a hot jet of pain seared through his wing and he squawked in agony and fury, instinctively twisting up, away from the danger. The damaged wing flapped jerkily as he struggled to gain height.

Nimlet watched him go, spitting out bits of feather in disgust. *Yuck! That's rank! Lucky and his stupid ideas!*

Down below, Lucky had easily grabbed the falling squirrel. She was skin and bone, not much bigger than him, and she was lying motionless on the branch—was she dead?

Nimlet landed with a *thud* by his side, looking very pleased with himself. But his expression changed when he saw the female. "She's not one of us!" he exclaimed.

"What d'you mean?"

"She's a Northend squirrel, Lucky! I've just risked tail and whisker for a Northend squirrel!"

"So what? You beat off a magpie! That was brilliant! Who cares what tree she came from?"

Nimlet shook his head. "Don't be stupid. Can't you see? She's not a Cloudfoot."

"So she's not worth rescuing?" Lucky couldn't believe it.

"She's not one of us!"

"Like me, then!"

"That's different—"

"No, it's not!" snapped Lucky. "Do I look like a Cloudfoot? No one thinks I'm a Cloudfoot!"

"I do," protested Nimlet.

"So what's the difference?" demanded Lucky. "At least she looks like you. No, hang on—she's not as ugly as you!"

"Ugly!"

"Ugly *stinking* Cloudfoot!"

"Stinking red *runt*!"

"Lousy fat *fart*!"

"Lousy mutant *tree-rat*!"

Lucky rose up, quivering with rage. "Call *me* a rat?"

There was dead silence. Then they started laughing. They would have carried on rolling around the branches, snorting and howling—but the little Northend squirrel was conscious now, and crying.

"What do we do?"

"I don't know!" said Nimlet. "Cloudfoot females aren't supposed to cry . . ."

Lucky plucked up courage and went over to the sobbing Northender. "Are you all right, ma'am?"

"No! Of course I'm not! That was horrible!" exclaimed the squirrel tearfully.

She pulled herself together and sat up shakily and Lucky saw what Nimlet meant. The spiky-haired female looked nothing like the sleek, well-fed Cloudfoots: She had a sharp muzzle and huge eyes. Her tail hair was sparse and straggly, but she was pretty, in a skinny sort of way.

"What Family are you?" She'd never seen a squirrel like him before.

"I'm Lucky, ma'am." What did she mean, Family?

"I'm not a 'ma'am'—don't you know me?"

Lucky shook his head—why should he know her?

"I am the Honorable Mistress Tarragon, beloved niece of Major Fleet, Protector and Great Leader of the Northend Family Fleet!" she declared. "You may address me as *Honorable Mistress*."

For a squirrel with a fancy name she looks like a mess, thought Lucky, but he tried again. "How can we help you, Honorable Mistress?"

"Take me home!" wailed the little squirrel, and burst into tears again.

"Okay! Okay!" said Lucky, panicked. *Anything* to stop her crying.

"Lucky, that's crazy! We can't take her back to the Northend—we've got to finish the Run!"

"What do you mean 'back to the Northend'?" Tarragon looked around in alarm and recognized none of the trees. "Where am I?"

"This is Cloudfoot Avenue, *Miss Fleet*, and we won't have any of your Northend nonsense here," said Nimlet sharply.

Tarragon backed away, appalled. The treacherous Cloudfoot enemy! "Ooh-ooh, I'm doomed!" she squealed dramatically.

"No, you're not. We rescued you!" said Nimlet crossly.

"But—but I thought there was a raid . . ." She screwed up her brow, trying to remember. It was so confusing. "I—I was high up—I was dizzy—and a bird came swooping down . . ."

"Yes," said Lucky patiently. "You were taken by a magpie, but Nimlet tackled him and I caught you."

Her huge dark eyes widened in amazement. "Mr. Nimlet—*you*? You fought off a bird?" She stood up, her tail flicking with excitement.

"Well, er, yes," said Nimlet, suddenly rather embarrassed.

"And I caught you," repeated Lucky, but the female ignored him.

"Mr. Nimlet, you are a true *warrior*! You are my *hero*!" She clasped her paws and looked up adoringly at the blushing Nimlet. "My uncle must reward you!"

"Stone the crows," muttered Lucky under his breath. *Any more of this*, he thought, *and I'm going to be sick*. "You didn't seem that grateful a moment ago," he said loudly.

"Ooh-ooh, Cloudfoots, I'm so sorry! I didn't mean to offend your Clan. My uncle thinks there's a raid—" A terrible thought suddenly hit her. "Oh no! I've got to go back right now! If I'm missing he might think you've taken me!"

"What, us?" said Lucky.

"No, silly! That I've been taken by the Cloudfoot raiding party. Don't you see? He has allies now—a huge army! They'll attack the Avenue!"

"Lucky, she's right. We have to get her back. And if there is a possibility of an attack we have to sound the alarm. Remember, it's what the Watch and Patrol is all about."

"Oh, fine," said Lucky sarcastically, "but is that before or after we finish the Final Run?"

"If the Honorable Mistress Tarragon is right, we have to move quickly."

Honorable Mistress Tarragon? What happened to *Miss Fleet*? wondered Lucky.

"We're going north, so we can take her to Ma Cloudfoot. She'll know what to do."

Tarragon skipped around, her tail swishing in delight. "Ooh-ooh, thank you, Mr. Nimlet—I can't tell you how grateful I am!"

Nimlet looked bashful and rather pleased.

"*Oh, Mr. Nimlet, I'm so grateful!*" mimicked Lucky. "How're we going to get to Ma Cloudfoot *and* finish the Run before sunset?"

"It's in the same direction. The Ma welcomes the runners at the Albion gates."

"Okay, okay," sighed Lucky, resigned. "Back up to the Canopy then."

"Oh no!" gasped Tarragon, horrified. "Please, not high up there—not near the birds! Surely there's another way?"

"Mazie's plan?" asked Nimlet.

"Guess so," said Lucky, grinning. "If you can fight off a magpie, you can fight off the Watch and Patrol—*my hero*!"

19

Second Daughter

The sun was setting over the Avenue and the Patrols seemed to have gone home. Moving quietly now was pointless; Lucky and Nimlet knew that they had to get back quickly to raise the alarm. Nimlet crashed tirelessly through the Mid-level branches and Lucky and Tarragon followed, struggling to keep up.

They came to a Watch Point, but the old squirrel there was far from alert. He'd been watching since dawn and was curled up in a tree trunk hollow, snoring loudly. The three squirrels scurried past him with no problem.

"I think that everyone's already been past," guessed Lucky correctly. "They're not on the lookout anymore!"

There was very little daylight left and Nimlet increased his speed. *We might*, he thought, *just make it in time.*

Lucky wasn't thinking about anything. He was concentrating all his efforts on leaping from branch to branch to keep up with his friend. Even Tarragon was ahead of him, but he didn't care—he just had to keep going.

The final six chestnut trees of the Avenue were in sight. Nimlet turned back to shout encouragement as Lucky screamed a warning—too late. A large, sleek Watch Squirrel dropped swiftly from above and pinned Nimlet to the branch.

"Keep going!" gasped Nimlet as he struggled under the weight of the Watch Squirrel. This was no dozing oldster; this was a real pro-Watcher, a mature and skilled fighter.

The Watch Squirrel moved to get a hold on Nimlet. They thrashed around frantically, hind legs pummeling and tails whiplashing from side to side. Nimlet broke free and the Watch Squirrel lunged and grabbed again.

Unbalanced, they both lost their hold, and Lucky and Tarragon watched in horror as the two crashed down through the branches. Lucky went to follow, but Tarragon put a restraining paw on his shoulder.

"We have to get to the Albion gates!" she said.

"That's my friend," Lucky snapped at the female. "We have to help him!"

"No, we have to get to the gates! That was what he said—remember?"

Lucky glared at her in disgust. She was right—and he really hated her for it.

They set off again through the branches, the sound of furious fighting fading into the distance. They were now very close to the Albion gates and a Cloudfoot female came into view. It was Second Daughter, Nimlet's mother. What a relief!

"Ma'am!" he called, bobbing respectfully.

"Lucky!" exclaimed Second Daughter, swiftly disguising her disappointment. How on earth had he gotten this far up the Avenue? She suddenly noticed his companion. *A Northender!* What was he doing with a Northend female? And . . . "Where is my son?"

"Nimlet is wrestling the final Watch Squirrel so that I can get to the Albion gates," said Lucky breathlessly. "This is Mistress Tarragon." The female bobbed gracefully. "She was taken by a magpie and we have to get her back home!"

"I see," said Second Daughter, her eyes narrowing and her devious mind working fast. "A Northend female in Cloudfoot space—this could start a war."

"Yes! We've got to get to the Ma."

"No! You must take Mistress Tarragon back to the Northend immediately. I will tell the Ma."

"But what about finishing the Run? What will the Instructor say?"

"Lucky," she said, fixing him with a beady eye, "I shall confirm you've finished the Run. You must go to the Northend quickly. Take the Ground-level path—it's quiet tonight."

"What about Nimlet?"

"I'll ask Ma Cloudfoot to send him after you to help. A large group of Patrol squirrels would look like a raiding party."

Lucky nodded in agreement; this was the sort of logical thinking that First Daughter had taught him.

"There is not a moment to lose." Second Daughter smiled kindly at them both. "Good-speed, Lucky, we are all depending upon you. Good-speed, Mistress Tarragon, may you store and survive."

"Mistress Cloudfoot," said Tarragon formally, "the Family Fleet thank you."

They leapt across the branches and were soon spiraling down the tree trunk out of sight.

Second Daughter watched them go, her false smile replaced by a sneer. *Pompous little Northend runt*, she thought. *The Family Fleet thank me, do they? I don't think so!*

20

Betrayal

The wrestling squirrels had fallen on the crisscross branches of the lower level. Winded and bruised, they still grappled tightly together.

Nimlet was struggling desperately to break free. *He's going to win*, he thought. *He's too strong!* He realized he had finally met his match.

The Watch Squirrel had been a wrestling champion before Nimlet was even out of the drey, and he was determined that this young upstart wasn't going to beat him! *Promotion!* he thought, as he slammed Nimlet down again. *He's gotten past the rest—he won't get past me. I've got my orders!* He was also frantic to beat Nimlet so he could go after the deformed "Lucky" animal. The Trial Instructor

had made his reasons very clear: "Not Cloudfoot material—
he must not be allowed to finish the Run, gentlemen." Even
Second Daughter had hinted at her support if he succeeded
in Casting Down Lucky.

No surprise they don't want a runt like that, the Watch
Squirrel thought. *A disgrace to the Watch and Patrol!* And who
was the female? A Northender spy? *I'll get them both—and
promotion for sure!* The Watch Squirrel redoubled his efforts.

Nimlet was really taking a beating now and he knew his
strength was failing; he was going to make a mistake sooner
or later, so he had to think of something—and fast. What
would Lucky do?

"I surrender!" yelped Nimlet, going limp on the branch.

"What?" exclaimed the Watch Squirrel, drawing back in
surprise.

Nimlet tore himself off the branch and tumbled to the
next level.

"You dirty motherless rat! That's against the rules!"

"What rules?" said Nimlet, who jumped to the trunk of
the next tree and spiraled swiftly upward.

"Come back, you coward!" demanded the Watch
Squirrel, shaking his fist as Nimlet disappeared above him.

"Okay," Nimlet shouted as he dove off the tree. The Watch Squirrel's nose hit the branch with a *thwack* as Nimlet landed on the squirrel's head. Nimlet leapt up and crashed off toward the Albion as fast as he could, before the dazed and moaning Watch Squirrel could recover.

The last light of day was fading, but there were no other squirrels between him and the Albion—he was going to make it! They were all going to make it! Wait until Lucky heard how he'd tricked the Watch Squirrel— what a laugh! The pretty Northend squirrel would be impressed too . . .

He could hear the sounds of other squirrels now, so he knew he was very near. Sure enough, there were groups of cadets with their proud families up ahead. Nimlet strained his eyes to see Lucky and cursed his shortsightedness. Then he saw First Daughter scurrying toward him. Lucky and Tarragon couldn't be far behind.

"Nimlet," cried First Daughter, "I'm so glad to see you! Where's Lucky?"

"Isn't he here?" He looked around wildly, completely confused.

"No, I've been frantic with worry. Everyone else has finished the Run. I thought you must have been caught at the ash trees. Why isn't he with you?"

"B-but he came on ahead!" stuttered Nimlet. "He has to be here. He came with Tarragon!"

"Who's Tarragon? Nimlet, what on earth are you talking about?!"

Before he could answer there was a great deal of hushing and shushing as Ma Cloudfoot and the Trial Instructor appeared to signal the end of the Run. "The Trials are over!" declared the Instructor. "These males who have finished the Run are no longer cadets—they have proved themselves worthy to join the Watch and Patrol. They are, as of today, official Defenders of the Cloudfoot Clan!"

A massive cheer went up throughout the trees. Nimlet and First Daughter were the only squirrels not rejoicing. This was a disaster! Lucky wasn't there, and now it was too late—he had failed the Final Run!

Second Daughter scurried up to their side. "Well, my son, it seems that I must congratulate you."

Nimlet looked at her blankly. What was the cause for celebration?

"Dear sister . . . I feel for you. What a pity that your

adopted son didn't finish the Run. Still, we didn't really expect him to, did we?" she said sweetly. "I wonder what could possibly have happened to him?" And with that she whisked away, a contented smile on her spiteful, treacherous face.

21

Major Fleet

Second Daughter's advice was good, thought Lucky. *It is quiet this evening, and much quicker at Ground-level. I hope Nimlet catches up soon.*

Tarragon kept on stopping, wide-eyed and trembling.

"Come on—we have to hurry," Lucky urged. "What's the matter?"

"I've never been down here before."

Lucky was surprised. "Haven't you foraged for food at Ground-level?"

"What a silly idea!" she said. "Honorable-born Fleets don't forage—we have common squirrels for that!"

"But you must have been taught the Knowledge?"

Tarragon had no idea what he was talking about. "Why should I need to know anything?" Her little face was screwed up in confusion.

Lucky had never heard anything so silly. "So you know the right thing to do, of course!"

"Oh, I know the right thing to do," she said brightly. "Trust and obey my uncle at all times, because he knows best."

"Well, that's not how the Cloudfoots see it—it's the Ma who knows best in the Avenue."

"A female? In charge?" exclaimed Tarragon. "Now that's *really* silly!" By this time they'd reached the first Northend trees and Tarragon immediately scurried up the trunk. "I can't carry on down there," she panted. "Please, let's go through the trees."

"Look," said Lucky, "I don't want to risk being attacked by one of your Northend soldiers. It's dark; they can't see us as easily on the ground. We need to get straight to your uncle and explain."

Tarragon sighed, but she came down to the ground again, looking nervously around.

"Don't worry, I'll protect you," said Lucky kindly.

Tarragon hid a smile. She could imagine the strong and handsome Mr. Nimlet protecting her—but this little squirrel with the strange ears? No!

The shadowy outline of the first Fleet Family trees appeared through the dark night and she heaved a sigh of relief. She was almost home and she felt a warm glow of excitement.

"We'll go straight to Uncle's drey," she declared, and scampered up the rough bark of an old sycamore tree.

Lucky followed more slowly and carefully. *We've rescued her, but the Northenders don't know that*, he thought. *I'm still a stranger in enemy trees.* He decided to hold back until Tarragon had told the whole story.

"Uncle!" she squeaked. "Uncle, I'm safe. The Cloudfoots rescued me and brought me back!"

In the dark tangle of the sycamore tree branches, the outline of a head appeared from out of the drey. "Tarragon?" said the Major. "Tooth and claw—I don't believe it!"

"Yes, it's me! Oh, dearest Uncle, you can't *imagine* how terrible it's been—" She stopped abruptly. The moon had risen above the tower blocks, illuminating the drey, and the furious look on the Major's face was clear to see.

"Has anyone seen you come here?" he demanded coldly.

"N-no," said Tarragon, confused. "Aren't you pleased to see me?"

"You simpering little fool," spat the Major. "Of course I'm not pleased to see you! Tomorrow we attack the Cloudfoots and you turn up—just in time to spoil my plan!"

"But the Cloudfoots didn't take me—they *rescued* me!"

"Pah! It doesn't matter who took you, it's the excuse I've been waiting for. Bracken and Glade are united behind me. With my Coppice allies we're finally strong enough to invade the Avenue."

"But you can't do that!" squealed Tarragon. "They're really nice!"

"Nice?" snarled the Major. "They're the enemy, you idiot! Get in the drey. I don't want you seen. Ever again—you'll ruin everything."

"No!" sobbed Tarragon, backing down the tree trunk. "No! No! No!"

"Don't force my hand, girl!" he declared. "Your parents got in my way, and I'll happily sacrifice you too!" He started to move threateningly toward her.

Lucky emerged swiftly from the shadows. He wrenched Tarragon's grip from the tree bark and held her dangling by the tail in midair. "You'll have to catch her first," he said cheerfully, and dove off the tree, dragging the terrified and screaming Tarragon after him.

Major Fleet was stunned—what on earth was that? It looked like no squirrel he'd ever seen. Were the Cloudfoots breeding monsters now? Still, no matter, the important thing was to dispose of Tarragon before she was seen.

The Families believed that the Cloudfoots had taken her and it was the perfect excuse to unite the Northenders in a war to conquer the Avenue.

To unite them all under *his* leadership as Supreme Commander.

22

Dogs and Foxes

Finlay and Eric were sitting comfortably on the bandstand in the middle of the Park. The moon rose over the tower blocks, picking out the grass and trees in silvery gray.

Eric enjoyed patrolling at night. There was a strong chance of spotting a fox up to no good and "apprehending" it. Finlay pointed out that chasing foxes *before* they'd done something wrong was not proper police procedure.

"Nah, that's dumb, Fin," said Eric, shaking his huge head, the studs and spikes on the hated harness sparkling in the moonlight. "Foxes are always up to no good, even if they don't look like they are!"

"Eric, this isn't the right attitude. Innocent until proven guilty—remember?"

"Yeah, but they're all thieves and liars—*you* said that!"

Finlay's reply was interrupted by the faint but unmistakable sound of an animal—female?—screaming in fright. Finlay and Eric stiffened, and their ears swiveled in unison toward the source of the sound. It came from the Northend trees.

"Sounds like squirrel," suggested Eric.

"Hmm . . . those Northenders are a quarrelsome lot," said Finlay. "It probably wouldn't hurt to trot over and take a look, eh?" They jumped from the bandstand and started off across the moonlit playing fields.

Reaching the branch safely, Tarragon could have burst into tears. Instead she was furious. "You—you—*Cloudfoot*!" she screeched. "Are you trying to kill us both?"

Lucky had almost dropped the struggling and screaming Tarragon. He'd only just swung her to safety at the very last minute. Now she wasn't even grateful! "No, *Honorable Mistress*, I'm trying to *save* you!" he said crossly. "But please yourself! You can go back to your *beloved* uncle, or you can come with me."

Tarragon heard the violent crashing sounds in the syca-more tree above. The Major was coming, and if he caught her . . . she was young and she was silly, but she wasn't stu-pid. "I think," she said, "I'll come with you."

They hit the ground running and headed swiftly back toward the Albion. Lucky spotted an animal in the dis-tance rushing toward them. *Tooth and whisker! If that's a Northender, we're done for.*

The shape got nearer and . . . *Thank goodness, it's Nimlet,* thought Lucky. *He's taken his time!* "You took your time!"

"Oh, thanks!" This wasn't the greeting Nimlet was expecting. "How was I supposed to find you?"

"What—?"

"Dogs!" cried Tarragon. She pointed toward the playing fields. The squirrels turned to run as Finlay and Eric trotted up. "Ooh-ooh, I know you! You're Mr. Finlay—and look! It's the fox with the pretty tail!"

"Hiya!" said Amber, emerging from the bushes.

Before Finlay could order Amber home, Lucky leapt over to the dog. "Mr. Finlay! We're under attack!"

"Lucky! What from?"

"Him," said Lucky, pointing toward the angry gray squir-rel crashing through the undergrowth toward them.

"Ah, I see," said Finlay. "Eric—"

"First bites?" challenged Eric to the fox cub.

146

"Good hunting!" grinned Amber. They raced off, the Staffy barking frenziedly, and the Major turned tail and frantically scrambled up a trunk. The animals jumped around the tree, their slavering jaws snapping at the air.

Dogs and foxes! The world's gone mad! Major Fleet thought as he rushed back to the Mid-levels. Still, *he* was safe; Tarragon and her Cloudfoot would be prey to the animals now. *Good riddance!* he thought, leaping back to his drey. *I'll mobilize my troops at once—we'll attack at first light!*

Eric and Amber returned, arguing hotly over who had gotten to the squirrel first.

"That's enough, you two," ordered Finlay crossly. "Now, what's going on? The Park isn't safe for squirrels at night. Get back to the Albion before any of your other *friends* turn up." He glared at Amber.

"Yes—and we have to be quick!" said Lucky. "The Northenders are planning to attack the Avenue and I have to warn the Ma!"

"Are you nuts?" exclaimed Nimlet. "You can't go back to the Avenue. You didn't finish the Run, so you'll be Cast Down!"

"No, Nim, it's okay! Didn't Second Daughter tell you?"

"Tell me what?" said Nimlet, confused. "My mother's said nothing."

"We met her," said Tarragon. "She told Lucky to take me straight home. But she promised to explain that he'd finished the Run, then send you after us!"

She wants Lucky Cast Down! thought Nimlet in horror. *She doesn't care what it takes! She'd even risk the safety of the Avenue to spite First Daughter.* He felt so ashamed that he could hardly look his friend in the eye.

"Lucky, I just guessed that you'd gone straight to the Northend," he said miserably. "My mother said nothing about seeing you. I'm so sorry—we all thought you'd failed."

"But that means that she didn't tell them about Tarragon either," said Lucky, horrified, "and there's going to be a raid!"

"I'll go back and warn them," declared Nimlet. "I've got to make this right!"

"No! We all go back. I don't look like a Cloudfoot, but they're my Clan and I *will* protect them!" Lucky pulled himself up to look as fierce as he could, daring them to disagree.

"Even if Ratter wants to throw you out?"

"Let him try!" declared Lucky.

Nimlet grinned and slapped him on the back. "Home to the Albion it is, then!"

23

Night Watch

In the first huge chestnut tree of the Avenue, a very angry squirrel with a swollen nose stood guard. Yesterday he'd been a renowned wrestling champion, expected to go far in the Cloudfoot ranks. Now he was demoted to corporal *and* night duty, a laughingstock among all the males. Beaten by a cadet! It was shameful.

He chittered and cursed quietly to himself as he forced his tired eyes to scan the Northend trees and the Ground-level between the Albion gates. *Pointless*, he thought, *there's no one out there*. But he was wrong about that.

Lucky, Nimlet, and Tarragon were hurrying back to the Avenue, with the two dogs guarding their backs.

Amber was tagging along, flatly refusing to go home. "Why can't I patrol too?"

"You're too young *and* you're a fox," growled Finlay.

"But I can help. Honest!" she argued.

"She only wants to be friends," said Tarragon.

"You and I," said Finlay, sighing, "need to have a serious talk about foxes."

The Albion gates came into view. "Lucky, it's nearly dawn and Eric and I have to get home to our humans," the German shepherd said. "They really can't be left on their own all night. Will you be all right?"

"Yes, thank you, Mr. Finlay."

"Tell the Ma we'll be back later, just in case this Northend business gets a bit . . . messy."

The squirrels watched as the dogs padded off, with Amber trailing behind, still arguing that she'd be a really *good* police fox. Honest.

"Right," said Lucky, "I have a plan. I'll go to First Daughter, and she can back us up. Nim, you and Tarragon get to the Ma. She might not believe you, but any chance of attack she'll ready the Watch and Patrol."

Nimlet nodded. The Ma would never take risks with the

defense of the Avenue, however unlikely their tale would sound. "Okay. I'm off."

"Lucky, be careful," said Tarragon. She darted forward and pecked him on the cheek. Lucky was stunned, and blushed from the tip of his nose to his tail.

Nimlet snorted and slapped his friend on the back, sending him staggering yet again. "Yeah, be careful—we don't want to lose you!"

Lucky slipped off through the undergrowth as fast as he could before they did anything else to embarrass him.

There was a faint glimmer of dawn beyond the tower blocks as Nimlet and Tarragon approached the Albion gates. It was enough light for the Watch Squirrel to spot the squirrels scurrying along the Ground-level. He immediately raised the alarm before careering down the tree to confront the two strangers.

Tooth and claw, they're not strangers, he thought, grinding his teeth. *This night gets worse.* But he had to make the traditional challenge. "Who steps into Cloudfoot space?"

"Greetings, Cloudfoot," declared Tarragon formally. "May you store and survive. I am the Honorable Mistress Tarragon Fleet, of the Northend Family Fleet, and this is my companion, Mr. Nimlet. We wish to request an audience with your Ma."

"Is that so?" snarled the squirrel.

Nimlet recognized him with a sinking heart. *Oh, nuts,* he thought, *of all the squirrels in all the trees, it had to be this one.*

"Ma Cloudfoot doesn't see *Northenders,*" spat the Watch Squirrel, "and she doesn't see cowards and cheats!" He glared at Nimlet, who bristled with rage.

Tarragon grabbed him by the arm. "Be nice!" she whispered.

Nimlet wasn't going to be nice. "You dirty runt!" he growled. "Who are you calling a coward?"

"Stop it, Mr. Nimlet!" said Tarragon, shocked. "You can't speak like that!"

"Yeah, *stop it, Mr. Nimlet!*" mocked the Watch Squirrel. "Be a nice little *pet* for the Northender. What sort of a pathetic animal are you?"

"The sort who left you beaten," declared Nimlet. "How's your nose today?"

They were eye to eye, and itching to fight. One more insult would tip the balance. But the alarm had woken the Trial Instructor, and he emerged furiously from his drey. "Mr. Nimlet! What do you think you're doing?"

"Sir!" said Nimlet, standing to attention. "This is the Honorable Mistress Tarragon Fleet and she has an urgent message for the Ma!"

With a dainty flourish of her tail, Tarragon made a polite bob to Ratter, who was completely taken aback. A Northend female? In Cloudfoot space? This was extremely irregular!

"Sir, my companion, Mr. Nimlet, speaks truly. The Avenue is in great danger of attack and we must warn the Ma," said Tarragon urgently.

The Trial Instructor snapped fully awake. Attack? "Ma'am, I shall escort you to the Meeting Drey immediately. Night Watch!" he ordered. "Get back to your post; I shall deal with you later. How dare you keep the Honorable Mistress waiting?"

The Watch Squirrel looked completely miserable and Nimlet almost felt sorry for him. But, passing by to follow Ratter, he caught curses that would curl Tarragon's tail. And a muttered threat that left no doubt. The squirrel wanted revenge.

I'd better mind my back, thought Nimlet. *That's a real enemy I've made today.*

24

The Meeting Drey

Nimlet and Tarragon spiraled up the trunk of the chestnut tree, following the Trial Instructor. *This is going okay*, thought Nimlet, starting to feel more cheerful. *Ratter seems to believe us—perhaps we can convince the Ma.* They reached the Mid-levels and scurried along the branches to the next tree.

The Trial Instructor took them to a large drey, the meeting place for the Ma and her Senior Daughters. This morning it was cold, dark, and deserted.

"Ma'am." He bobbed to Tarragon. "Would you honor me by waiting here while I get word to the Ma?" He swished his tail in a dashing manner and leapt out of the drey.

Tarragon smiled as she watched him go; these Cloudfoots were all so nice!

It was not long before the Ma entered with her Attendants. Ratter had swiftly returned to the Albion gates after alerting her. The young Northender's story might be stuff and nonsense, but he was taking no chances with the defense of the Avenue.

Both Nimlet and Tarragon politely bobbed low as the Ma settled on her haunches. As they rose, Second Daughter entered the drey and Nimlet willed her to look him in the eye. *It could—it* could *all be a mistake*, he thought, desperately wanting it to be true. But his mother sat by the side of the Ma and ignored him. Nimlet's heart sank.

The old Ma had not been pleased to be summoned and her face was stony. "Well?" she demanded.

Nimlet hung back, quite overwhelmed by her presence. Tarragon, to her credit, did not show how nervous she really was. She stepped forward with her head held high and declaimed loudly, "Great Ma of the Cloudfoot Clan! I am the Honorable Mistress Tarragon Fleet of the North—"

"Oh, get on with it, girl!" snapped the Ma. "Yes. Yes, we know who you are. What we don't know is what you want."

"Mistress, I want to warn you. My uncle, head of the Family Fleet, is planning an attack on Cloudfoot Avenue."

The Ma's whiskers flared. "What makes you say this, girl?"

"Mistress, I heard him say so."

The Ma's ill-tempered eyes narrowed as Tarragon explained her rescue from the magpie and the Watch Squirrel's surprise attack. "But Mr. Nimlet fought him off bravely so that Mr. Lucky and I could get to the Albion and raise the alarm."

"Really?" said the Ma sharply. "So why have we not already been warned?"

Tarragon hesitated. She looked at Nimlet and then at Second Daughter. Would the Ma believe her? *I wish Lucky was here*, she thought. She took a deep breath and then explained, "Because, mistress, we met Nimlet's mother and she told us to go straight to the Northend. So we did, and my uncle . . . um . . . wasn't very pleased to see me. I was missing, so he had his excuse to start a war. He was very angry that I'd come back."

"I see," said the Ma, turning to Second Daughter. "Well, what have you got to say?"

Nimlet held his breath. One last chance? She'd lied before; would she lie again?

Second Daughter smiled and spread her paws in a convincing display of amused confusion. "I have no idea what to say. The poor child has obviously had a terrible time and must be in shock. I have never seen her before in my life."

Why won't she tell the truth? thought Nimlet miserably. But in his heart he knew. He knew she was lying to protect herself. That she'd betrayed them all. That she was no longer his mother.

The Ma frowned; this was extremely irritating. Then she muttered an order to a Daughter Attendant, who disappeared swiftly into the Mid-levels. The Ma regarded them all with the same cold contempt, but her gaze came to rest on Nimlet.

Oh no! thought Nimlet. *Please not me! Not now.*

"Cadet." She gestured. "Come here."

He came stumbling forward and made the clumsiest bob the Ma had ever seen. It almost made her smile, but not quite.

"So you are Mr. Nimlet," she mused, "the champion wrestler?"

"Y-yes, ma'am." He screwed up his eyes, willing his tail to stop shaking.

"You must be an excellent wrestler to beat the final Watch Squirrel."

Nimlet nodded dumbly; he only hoped she hadn't heard how he'd beaten him.

"And you did this so that Mr. Lucky and Mistress Tarragon could get to the Albion gates?"

"Yes, ma'am." This was going better; she seemed to understand.

"So the Watch Squirrel spotted all three of you?"

"Oh, yes!" said Nimlet.

"Excellent," said the Ma, just as the Watch Squirrel was brought in. "We can now proceed." She fixed the unhappy demoted animal with her beady eyes. "Corporal, do you recognize this male?"

The Watch Squirrel looked at Nimlet with utter loathing. He spoke through gritted teeth. "Yes, ma'am, he is the cadet who got past me during the Final Run."

"Splendid," said the Ma. They were getting somewhere now. "And do you recognize this female?" She gestured toward Tarragon.

"No, ma'am. I'm sorry, ma'am."

Tarragon and Nimlet gasped in unison.

Second Daughter hid her malicious little smile. "Did you not see her with Mr. Lucky?"

"I saw neither of them, ma'am. The first I knew was when she turned up at the Albion gates—with him." He glared at Nimlet.

The Ma stood up. She was so furious she could hardly speak. "We are returning to our drey. Keep these animals under guard until we have the time and inclination to deal with them."

Tarragon stepped forward to protest, but the Ma held up her paw. "No! No more lies and nonsense! We Have Had Enough!"

"But, ma'am," interrupted Nimlet desperately. "Lucky can prove it—he heard the Major's plan!"

"Mr. Lucky," said the Ma coldly, "has failed the Final Run and is Cast Down from the Avenue. He is no longer a Cloudfoot and no squirrel will speak his name in these trees again!"

Nimlet and Tarragon stared in speechless horror as the Ma turned to go. But her exit was blocked as a breathless and disheveled Patrol Leader staggered into the drey.

"Ma'am!" He drew a deep jagged breath. "The Northenders, ma'am! There is an army at the Albion gates—we are under attack!"

25

The Albion Gates

Word of the attack reached First Daughter's home-tree moments after Lucky had arrived. "I must go and help the Ma immediately," she declared.

Lucky and Mazie moved to go with her.

"What do you think you two are doing?" First Daughter demanded. "Miss Trimble, *you* will ensure that Lucky stays here safely in the drey. I want *both* of you out of sight until this is over." Lucky started to protest but First Daughter silenced him. "Lucky, you are no longer a member of the Clan. Until I get to the Ma and explain, you are in danger. It would be the duty of any Cloudfoot to Cast you Down if they saw you, understand?"

Lucky nodded miserably as First Daughter leapt out of the drey, and the two squirrels watched her disappear through the branches at breakneck speed.

"Hmm," mused Mazie. "So, my orders are to keep you in the drey?"

"And we have to keep out of sight," added Lucky.

"So, if I couldn't keep you in the drey and we both stayed out of sight, then we wouldn't *exactly* be disobeying orders, would we?" suggested Mazie.

"You'd do that?" Lucky was amazed. Mazie never disobeyed orders!

"D'you *want* to sit here while the Avenue's under attack?"

"No! I want to find Nimlet and Tarragon! But they could be anywhere."

"Oh, that's easy," said Mazie. "If they went to see the Ma there's only one place they'd be, and that's the Meeting Drey."

"Great! Let's go," said Lucky. "But we mustn't be seen. I don't want to 'disobey orders'!"

Old Ma Cloudfoot had more flecks of white in her fur than gray. No one knew how many leaf-falls she had seen, and no squirrel would dare to ask. She had come into the Meeting

Drey moving slowly and stiffly. But at the news of an attack, she moved like a young cadet. Storming over to the gates, she gathered Daughters and barked orders to the Watch.

First Daughter joined them as they sped toward the Albion gates. She told a grim-faced Ma that Lucky had reached her, confirming the Northend plot and Second Daughter's treachery. Nimlet and Mistress Tarragon had been telling the truth.

Second Daughter, strangely enough, had slipped away, depriving a furious Ma of judgment and justice. *If that traitor ever steps foot in my trees again*, she thought savagely, *I will Cast her Down myself—With No Mercy!* She bristled with rage and leapt even faster through the trees.

The Ma arrived at the Albion and gazed with horror at the scene of confusion and carnage. The attackers were already swarming up through the first chestnut tree into the Avenue. "Where is the Trial Instructor?" she demanded.

Then she saw him. Ratter's drey was surrounded by a mob of lean and vicious Northend troops. The old warrior was fighting valiantly, furious that his Watch and Patrol had been caught unawares. He lunged and spun at the enemy squirrels coming from all sides. No Northender would live to set foot on his home-tree!

The Ma scanned the trees. How many were there? Too many! On every branch outnumbered troops battled the

Northend swarm and injured Cloudfoots crashed blood-stained through the branches—they never reached the ground.

Birds swooped out of the sky, their metallic-black snapping wings propelled beak and claw, and there were desperate screams as falling squirrels were borne away by the delighted hungry hunters. "Ca-ca-cack!" *A feast! A feast!*

They have a plan, thought the Ma bitterly as she watched the well-drilled forces of Fleet and Coppice. The Patrol Leader was right. *This* is *more than one Family, and still they come!* Across the gate poured squirrels from Glade and Bracken. It was not an organized advance, but they were a large and angry mob.

The news had spread to all the Northend Families—how dare the Cloudfoots steal one of their Honorable females? Their trees would be forfeit and their males Cast Down! Together they could take the lush and plentiful Avenue—and never be hungry again. It was a cry to arms few Families could resist, and Northenders rushed to join the throng.

The Ma watched, stony-faced and calculating, as the invading hordes poured over the third chestnut. She turned to her Daughter Generals and ordered a retreat.

"No, ma'am!" spluttered the Patrol Leader before he could stop himself. "We must fight!"

"Fool!" snapped the Ma. "Can't you see we are outnumbered and unprepared? Retreat to the sixth chestnut, we shall hold them there—and rally all the Watch and Patrol. We shall have need of soldiers."

The Patrol Leader was Cloudfoot material through and through. He would never disobey the Word of Ma. But as he rushed through the trees, ordering the retreat, he spotted the Trial Instructor in the distance, still defending his drey. He was surrounded by the mauled and bloody bodies of Northend troops, but the tide of squirrels hadn't stopped. More shapes were scurrying across the Albion gates and spiraling up the Avenue trees. Retreat would be unthinkable for the Instructor. The old warrior was going to be Cast Down—alone and abandoned by his Clan.

That, thought the Patrol Leader through gritted teeth, *is not going to happen on my Watch!* He gathered all his strength and leapt skillfully through the branches. Enemy claws scrabbled to catch him, but he was the best of the Cloudfoots and could fly through the familiar trees faster than any Northender. He reached the old Trial Instructor's side just in time—Ratter was pinned down by two ragged Northenders who were going in for the kill.

The Patrol Leader wrenched the first Northender from Ratter and tossed him off the chestnut.

The second squirrel lunged at him with teeth bared and claws outstretched, screeching in rage for his fallen comrade. The two warriors crashed furiously together: a thrashing many-limbed beast, twisting and turning in a frantic effort to deal a death blow. The Northender came out on top and the Patrol Leader squealed as his enemy lunged forward with outstretched claws. Suddenly the Northend squirrel went limp as his body was shoved aside by Ratter.

"Stranglehold," said the Trial Instructor drily. "Not often used in battle conditions."

The Patrol Leader looked at him, dumbstruck. Was this really the time for a lecture? "Sir," he said urgently, "the Ma has ordered a retreat, to regroup at the sixth chestnut."

"Indeed?" said Ratter. "Then we must obey the Word of Ma."

26

Fight Like a Cloudfoot

Your parents got in my way . . . The Major's words echoed around and around in Tarragon's head. She paced the Meeting Drey, her face screwed up in concentration. Got in his way? What did he mean?

She tried to remember . . . *I'll happily sacrifice you too* . . . And he would, wouldn't he?

Your parents got in my way . . .

But he'd tried to save them from a Cloudfoot attack, hadn't he? That was the story he told. He'd become Head of the Family, a hero and her protector!

But the Cloudfoots weren't murderers, they were nice! Why would they attack the Northend anyway?

And if the Cloudfoots didn't kill her parents . . .

Tarragon suddenly remembered the corporal's old grand-mother, and her sad little gift. She'd been afraid . . . they were *all* afraid . . . of *him*. A hot, sickly rush of understanding ran from whisker to tail. She shuddered.

How stupid I've been, she thought.

Nimlet sat near the mouth of the drey wrapped in his own misery. *We're at war. Lucky is banished. All because of* her *lies*, he thought bitterly. *I know she never liked me much, but how could she* do *this? Lucky's my only friend, and I've got to get out of here and find him. We could leave the Avenue together!*

He crept to the entrance and peeked over the parapet. The Watch Squirrel stood on the branch, blocking any escape. *He'd love me to try and get out*, thought Nimlet. *Any excuse to Cast me Down. There must be another way.*

He started to move around the walls, pushing at the woven twigs. At the back of the dark drey they felt softer . . . and furrier? Nimlet leapt back in surprise as Lucky's head erupted through the wall.

"Stop pushing, you idiot," he said, spitting out bits of twig. "I'm trying to get in!"

"Lucky! How did you find us?"

"Mazie knew where you'd be." He wriggled around the gap in the twigs. "I can't make it any bigger, so you can't get out this way."

"We can't get out the front. The Watch Squirrel's on guard."

"The angry one with the swollen nose? Nice one, Nim!"

"Yeah, well, he's not moving. Ma's orders."

"Mr. Lucky! What's happening at the Albion? Are the Cloudfoots winning?" Tarragon asked.

"I don't know—" Lucky stopped. "Are you okay?" Tarragon looked very strange and . . . flushed.

"We've got to get out," she said urgently. "We've got to get to the Albion!"

"Okay," said Lucky, his head disappearing back through the hole.

The Watch Squirrel had been on duty for hours and could hardly stand to attention. Only cold fury was keeping him upright. He'd followed Second Daughter's orders as a dutiful soldier, but knew he'd taken the wrong branch. *The Avenue's under attack and I'm stuck here!* He ground his teeth in frustration. *I should be at the Albion!*

The first stone hit him sharply on the ear. The second

bounced off his already tender nose. He gave a yelp of pain and looked around wildly. Was it a Northender? Then he spotted Lucky dancing on a slender branch above. The *mutant* was hurling pebbles and insults down at him—and the insults were getting ruder and nastier.

His final taunt hit the spot: No one should use those words about someone's mother.

"No one calls my mother that!" screamed the Watch Squirrel, angrily moving from the mouth of the drey. He looked up at Lucky and furiously shook his fist. "Come down and fight like a Cloudfoot, you dirty red runt!"

"But he's not a Cloudfoot, is he?" said Mazie, dropping lightly down behind him. Surprised, the exhausted male spun around off balance, and she easily pushed him off the branch. He fell screaming through the air. When he hit the ground there was silence—and he didn't move at all.

Bud and branch! thought Mazie, amazed at what she'd done. *I think my chances of promotion are ruined!*

The stunned Watch Squirrel shook himself awake with a whimper. Every limb protested and his head throbbed. He staggered to his feet, scanning the branches in vain for Lucky and Mazie, but they had gone.

The squirrels traveled high above the Mid-levels to keep out of sight. But the trees were deserted—every Cloudfoot was at the Albion.

They heard the angry cry of battle long before they reached the chestnuts. Soon they were close enough to see the violently shaking branches, which were alive with squirrels rolling and writhing together in combat. Wood cracked and splintered as they crashed through the Mid-levels.

It was hard to make out what was happening amid the noise and frantic action. But Nimlet's hearing was much better than his sight, and he caught fragments of the Daughter Generals' shouted orders on the wind, and stiffened in horror. "They're retreating! I don't believe it; they're calling for a retreat!"

"It's worse than that," said Tarragon flatly.

"What could be worse than that?" demanded Lucky. How could she be so stupid?

"There are squirrels from every Northend Family here in your trees," said Tarragon.

"So?" said Nimlet.

"Don't you see, Cloudfoots? *Every* Northend Family! My uncle has succeeded. He has a united army at last. He *will* take your Avenue."

27

Fallen

F inlay!"

The old dog cocked his ear and opened one eye. His human was calling. *Hmm*, thought Finlay, *he doesn't sound very happy.*

"Finlay—come here *now*!"

Finlay rose stiffly to his feet from the rug in front of the fire—he'd been deeply asleep for hours. He had a quick stretch and a scratch, and then padded out to the hallway. George stood by the open door.

"Look!" demanded the human, pointing to his Land Rover parked on the road. "The cheek of it! Unbelievable! Finlay, see it off."

There, sitting on the hood of the car cleaning her paws, was Amber. "Hiya!" She beamed.

What does she want now? thought Finlay crossly. "I'm going to pretend to chase you up the road," he growled, "then you can tell me why you're here—and it had better be good!" He launched himself forward and put on a good show for George, barking fiercely.

Amber leapt off the car and fled.

Finlay stopped halfway up the road, panting heavily. "All right, that's far enough." He didn't like to admit it, but he really couldn't run as fast as he used to. "What were you doing outside my house?" he demanded. "In fact, how did you even know it *was* my house?"

"Smelled ya!" said Amber smugly. "Front gate's got your mark all over it—and the lamppost's a dead giveaway. Told you I'd be a good police fox. I can track any scent trail *and* I've got powers of detection!"

"Oh, really?" said Finlay.

"Yeah! And I've detected that there's something going wrong with your squirrel friends. I think you and Mr. Eric might like to take a look."

Finlay couldn't believe his eyes when he reached the Albion. The sun was just setting, but Northenders were still scurrying across the gates to climb up the first chestnut. There didn't seem to be any Cloudfoots in the trees at all. Where was the Ma?

"Blimey, looks like they've been 'avin' a right scuffle," said Eric, pointing to some scraps of fur that had once been on a squirrel.

"Yeah, they were fighting in this tree earlier," said Amber. "But I did manage to stop the birds getting some of them."

"You *saved* squirrels?" said Finlay, amazed.

"Well, it was good fun chasing the birds off—and you *did* say we were supposed to be friends. So what are you going to do now?"

"Now?" said Finlay grimly. "Now we're going to find out if there's any chance of stopping this slaughter."

Surely the Northenders can't win? thought Mazie. She peered over the treetops, straining in the failing light to make sense of the action. The Daughter Generals were holding off the enemy, as the defeated Watch and Patrol stumbled back to the sixth chestnut. More Cloudfoot reinforcements were arriving from the Avenue to join the Ma and hold the line.

Yes, that was it. She understood now. They were going to make a stand at the sixth chestnut.

She recognized Ratter and the Patrol Leader, brutally forcing their way into the crush of Northend troops. They were going to the rescue of small bands of Cloudfoots, who were struggling to retreat. But they were only two against many. As soon as one Northender fell, another took his place: again and again.

They're outnumbered, she thought. *There are too many of them!*

Lucky's sudden cry of alarm cut through her thoughts. "Look! Up in the fifth chestnut—it's First Daughter!" He pointed wildly to the tree.

There was First Daughter, trapped and cut off by the advancing army. Bands of ragged Northenders from Bracken and Glade were swarming around the lower branches. They had not spotted her, but they would very soon.

"I have to rescue her!" cried Lucky in distress, starting forward.

Nimlet grabbed him by the arm. "Lucky, you won't stand a chance," he urged. "First Daughter wouldn't want you to."

"But—but—she's a *mother* to me!" he sobbed.

"Lucky might not stand a chance," said Mazie grimly to Nimlet, "but you and I just might."

Lucky looked in confusion from one friend to another. He didn't want to lose them either. What were they to do?

"Ooh-ooh, no!" cried Tarragon, pointing to the chestnut tree. "It's too late!"

A group of ragged Bracken squirrels had spotted First Daughter and were climbing up the trunk, evil in their sharp, hungry faces. This would be good sport and an easy kill.

First Daughter drew herself up proudly on the branch, her tail held high. She could smell their wickedness, but she would not run. She would not give them the pleasure of a hunt.

The Northenders reached the spar of her branch just as two Cloudfoots leapt skillfully from the fourth chestnut and landed with a thud on the branch before her. First Daughter hardly recognized them—Ratter's coat was a bloody stained mess, and the Patrol Leader had lost part of an ear. They turned snarling upon the startled Northenders, who dropped back at once.

"You will let us pass!" demanded Ratter.

The leading Bracken soldier grinned nastily. "*Granddad* wants to pass—not askin' very nice, is he?"

"Nah! Ask us *nicely*, Granddad," taunted another, "and we might only hurt you a bit!" The soldiers snickered at this witty response.

"That was not a request," said Ratter coldly. "*That* was an order."

Tails thrashing and hissing with rage, the two Cloudfoots plunged down upon the enemy, claws outstretched and teeth bared. Lucky watched in awe as the two warriors viciously forced the Northenders back to the lower branches. They had the height advantage and they would defend their Cloudfoot Daughter to the death.

"Get to safety, ma'am!" shouted the Trial Instructor.

My brave friends, thought First Daughter, *Good-speed to you both*. She raced along a slender spar and, with all the strength she could summon, launched herself into the air toward the sixth chestnut.

Lucky gasped and Mazie stiffened. It was too far—she'd never make it!

First Daughter arced through space and dove. Tail flicking frantically, she aimed for a branch and just caught the tip. The wood bowed and she lost her hold.

"No!" cried Lucky.

She fell farther, slowing her fall by catching the branch tips—but she was going to hit Ground-level.

"The Northenders will catch her!"

"No, look! It's Mr. Finlay!" Mazie pointed.

As First Daughter fell to the foot of the sixth chestnut, Finlay and Eric charged up to the base of the tree, scattering the Northend troops. Amber ran around them snapping happily, bits of tail-fur hanging from her jaws. Good hunting!

Finlay gently carried First Daughter over to the trunk and she climbed slowly to safety. Lucky and Mazie hugged each other in relief and delight.

But it was not yet over.

The Northenders' easy sport had turned into a bloody skirmish and they screamed for help from their Family below. More Bracken squirrels spiraled up the fifth chestnut toward Ratter and the Patrol Leader. Already surrounded, the two Cloudfoots would soon be hopelessly outnumbered and overpowered.

"Patrol Leader!" gasped Ratter, kicking a Northender away. "I order you to retreat." He spun around and caught another Northender with a cutting upsweep.

The Patrol Leader was backing up along a branch, holding off two snarling males. "No, sir!" he panted. "I'm not leaving you!" He twisted one Northender off the branch and stunned the other with a dropkick.

"I've had my day," growled the old warrior, "and you will have yours. Live to serve the Ma and defend the Avenue. Retreat *now*, Patrol Leader—that is an order!"

"The Patrol Leader is leaving!" cried Nimlet, horrified. "He's leaving Ratter to be Cast Down!"

"No," said Mazie, who had judged rightly that only one squirrel stood a chance of survival. "Ratter must have ordered him to go—the Patrol Leader would never desert the Trial Instructor."

The old warrior was almost hidden now beneath a writhing mass of furious Northend troops, swarming up the trunk. But he had not stopped fighting. Enemy squirrels were still screaming in pain as Ratter went down—dying as he had lived: a true Cloudfoot defender of the Avenue.

It was finally over. The sickened and stunned squirrels could see the Patrol Leader and First Daughter reunited with the Ma on the sixth chestnut. But of Ratter there was no trace. The Trial Instructor was Fallen.

The four young squirrels watched helplessly as every able-bodied squirrel, and a few who weren't, gathered to defend the sixth chestnut. From the youngest cadets to veteran oldsters, every Cloudfoot had been called to arms. Finlay, Eric, and Amber patrolled the battle line, keeping the Northenders from attacking at Ground-level.

"We should join the battle," urged Nimlet. "Not hide up here!"

"I have a better idea," declared Tarragon.

"You?" exclaimed Mazie. "What d'you know about battles?"

"I've had history lessons," said Tarragon primly. "I know all about battles!"

"Mistress Tarragon," said Mazie, surprisingly patiently. "This isn't the same. You know nothing of strategy and tactics."

"Or fighting," added Nimlet.

"No, but I know about my Family—and I have a plan!" This was exciting; she'd never had a plan before!

They all looked doubtful.

"What is this plan, Honorable Mistress?" asked Lucky kindly.

"Ooh-ooh! It's *ever* so clever!" said Tarragon. "And it goes like this . . ."

28

The Sixth Chestnut

Ma Cloudfoot was very angry—angry with herself. Never in Cloudfoot history had the Northenders taken the Albion. The Trial Instructor and many fine Defenders had Fallen. Her Second Daughter had betrayed them all. She should have trusted the Northend female. *I am not fit to be called the Ma*, she thought bitterly.

She sent First Daughter back to the Meeting Drey to collect the youngsters.

But it was empty and, to First Daughter's horror, so was her home-drey. News came that Second Daughter and the Watch Squirrel had been spotted fleeing the Avenue toward the Good Shepherd. But of Lucky, Mazie, Nimlet, and Tarragon there was no sign.

The battered and exhausted Cloudfoot males evacuated the chestnuts. A group of valiant Daughters took their place, keeping the invaders at bay. They fought to the bitter end, and one by one were Fallen. Finlay and Eric saved those they could, and Amber harried the swooping crows and magpies.

It bought the Cloudfoot Clan enough precious time to regroup, and a horde of Cloudfoot squirrels was now gathered on every branch of the sixth and final chestnut. The Northenders could advance no farther.

But as night drew in, more squirrels from Northend Families joined Major Fleet's troops and the Albion was occupied by the enemy. As the Ma gazed out at the invaders, she realized the chances of holding off a united Northend army were slim: very slim indeed.

They will attack again at dawn, she thought.

Light broke through the cold misty trees. As the Cloudfoots gathered to face the enemy, a low murmur of horror ran through the Clan. Hanging from the nearest branches of the fifth chestnut were the Fleet Family troops, and next to the Major stood . . . Nimlet.

The Ma could hardly believe her eyes. Betrayed by the mother *and* the son! She called for a parley.

"Mr. Nimlet, what do you think you are doing?" she demanded sternly from the branches of the sixth chestnut.

"I don't answer to you!" declared Nimlet. "I don't answer to any Cloudfoot. You are no longer my Clan—I have joined the Northenders!"

The Northend squirrels chittered and jeered, stamping their feet as the Cloudfoots looked on in dismay.

"Great Ma!" called the Major with a sneer. "Mr. Nimlet thinks I should ask for my niece back—before our army invades and we take her by force."

"Northender, we do not have your female," said the Ma, facing him defiantly.

"You lie," snarled the Major, his tail thrashing wildly. "See how the treacherous Cloudfoots lie!" he proclaimed to the surrounding Northend mob, who stamped and hissed in agreement.

"No," came a clear voice from above them. "She is not lying." Lucky stepped out from the high branches of the fifth chestnut Canopy and dove gracefully down to Nimlet's side. "There is your Honorable female!"

Tarragon emerged into full view above them, with Mazie

at her side. There was a sharp intake of breath from the Fleet squirrels, who recognized her immediately.

"You interfering runt!" growled the Major, lunging at Lucky.

But Nimlet was ready, and swiftly swung him around in an armlock. The Major's troops moved menacingly toward them, but Lucky held up his paw and declared loudly, "Listen to the truth from Mistress Tarragon Fleet!"

Tarragon dove down to the branch beside Lucky and made a graceful bow to all the Northenders around her. Many Fleets bobbed in formal response. War was no excuse to ignore good manners, and she *was* their Honorable Mistress.

"Fellow Northenders," she cried, "you have been deceived and badly used. I was not taken by the Cloudfoots—but *by a hunting bird*!" There was a collective cry of surprise. Just the effect she'd wanted! "I was rescued by these brave Cloudfoots"—she gestured toward Lucky and Nimlet—"who returned me to the Northend."

Northenders were chittering frantically to each other now. The Cloudfoots had *rescued* their Honorable Mistress?

"Don't listen to this foolish female," shrieked Major Fleet. "She has gone mad!"

"No," declared Tarragon, flourishing her tail dramatically. "It is you who are mad—mad for power!" She was really enjoying this now. "Fellow Northenders, I *was* returned home—but my uncle would have killed me, just as he did my parents, rather than see his chance for warfare spoiled!"

The Northenders were shaking their heads and chattering angrily. Was this true? They had been tricked! Groups of Glade and Bracken squirrels started to melt silently away into the trees.

"Comrades!" cried the Major, desperately trying to free himself from Nimlet's grip. "What does it matter? See what our united armies have achieved! Stay with me and we will conquer the whole Avenue!"

But it was too late. The allied Families were already disbanding; only the Family Fleet troops remained, and they were muttering mutinously. This was not honorable warfare.

The Major finally tore himself free from Nimlet and turned to his troops. "We *shall* hold these trees!" he ordered. "We need no other Northend help. This will be *my* territory!"

"Major Fleet!" The old Ma's voice rang out over the branches. "The time has come for retreat, and there has been enough bloodshed. Believe me, we will fight your troops till the last squirrel standing if you do not withdraw."

"There will be no retreat," declared the Major. "Not while I am leader of this Family!"

"In that case," declared Tarragon, "I challenge your leadership!"

The Northenders gasped in amazement—a female leader? It was unheard of!

Major Fleet laughed out loud. "Now I know you're mad!" He turned to his troops. "Seize them—they will be Cast Down!"

"No!" called Tarragon with a flourish of her tail. "Would you ignore tradition? Any Family leader can be challenged by an Honorable squirrel—and I make the Challenge!"

"That's true, mistress," said one of the Fleet soldiers, completely flustered. "But it has never been a . . . er . . . female."

"If the Cloudfoots have a female leader, so can the Northenders!" proclaimed Tarragon.

"This is absurd," sneered the Major. "You cannot challenge me. The tradition requires single combat—winner takes all. How can you possibly fight me?"

"*I* do not intend to fight you," said Tarragon primly. "I have a Champion."

"Oh, really," said Major Fleet. "And who is that?"

There was a pause as the Northenders looked around expectantly, waiting for the chosen Fleet warrior to appear.

Tarragon smiled sweetly. "My Champion," she declared dramatically, "is Mr. Nimlet!"

29

The Challenge

Lucky rounded furiously on Tarragon. "You idiot! You never said that was part of your plan! What're you doing?"

"You mustn't speak to an Honorable squirrel like that," she said primly. "I really think you should calm down."

"Calm down? Calm down? You've just volunteered my friend for a fight to the death!" He turned on Nimlet. "Did you know about this?"

"Er . . . no, but—"

"This is completely nuts!"

"Look, Lucky," said Nimlet reasonably. "The Major isn't going to retreat like the rest of them. There'll be many more

Cast Down squirrels today if I don't defeat him. I'm honored to be Mistress Tarragon's Champion."

"There's no point in being *honored*," spat Lucky, "if you're dead!"

At that moment a young Fleet soldier stepped forward and announced that they should leave the branch; the leader of the Family Fleet was ready for the Challenge. Nimlet readied himself.

He's not going to change his mind, thought Lucky. *I can't stop him and he is right—Cloudfoot lives will be saved if he wins.* But at that moment, the only life Lucky cared about was Nimlet's.

"Nim," he whispered urgently as they passed. "Don't fight like a Cloudfoot."

Nimlet nodded. He understood.

The Challenge began with the soldier holding Major Fleet and Nimlet apart. "Gentlemen, you may fight—*now*!" He dropped swiftly off the branch and the two males crashed together. They were well-matched in size—the Major was large for a Northender and just as strong as Nimlet.

The two gray bodies whipped around and around, a thrashing, spinning ball of tooth and claw. Major Fleet was a skilled and ruthless fighter and he was fueled with fury. His plans had been ruined and these Cloudfoots would pay! He lunged and spun, desperate to close in for the kill, but Nimlet matched his every move.

Lucky, from the viewing branch above, could see that his friend was cleverly keeping one step ahead of the furious Fleet male. But how long could he keep it up? Both were moving with dizzying speed, each screeching in anger and pain. They started to slip and slide, struggling to keep a grip.

Suddenly Nimlet seemed to lose his hold and stumbled backward, his arms flailing desperately. The Major reared up with a look of triumph on his face and prepared to pounce.

But the trick left him exposed. Nimlet kicked upward with all the strength in his hind legs and the Fleet male went sprawling. Nimlet leapt onto the animal and got him firmly into a choke hold.

"Now," panted Nimlet, "I might not fight like a Cloudfoot, but I follow the Word of Ma. Our aim is not the

Falling—we only Cast Down our enemy if he will not surrender. What do you say, Northender?"

The surrounding Northend troops were chattering in confusion. Why hadn't the Cloudfoot gone for the kill? He was clearly the winner!

Tarragon came scurrying onto the branch with Lucky close behind her. "Nimlet!" she cried urgently. "You must finish it—only one challenger can survive!"

"Enough squirrels have died," said Nimlet, wearily struggling to his feet. "I don't want to be a killer. It's not the Cloudfoot way."

"Then you Cloudfoots are fools!" came a voice from behind him.

Major Fleet had pulled himself upright. He lunged forward, and before Lucky could stop him, he had grabbed Tarragon by the neck and held her dangling in the air. "A step nearer," he growled, "and I Cast her Down!"

One glance passed between the friends, and Lucky dove off the tree to the branches below.

"Ha! Fools *and* cowards!" crowed the Major, watching Lucky go.

"Put her down," urged Nimlet. "Surrender now and you can leave Cloudfoot space unharmed."

"Unharmed!" the Major spat in disgust. "You Cloudfoots aren't real squirrels—you *cowards* have no stomach for true combat!" He dangled the struggling Tarragon farther out into space and shook her roughly. "Want the simpering little fool?" he taunted. "Come and get her—you fat, motherless Cloudfoot *rat*!"

That was enough for any squirrel. With a roar of fury, Nimlet hurled himself at the Fleet male, and the Major flung Tarragon off the branch. She spiraled screaming through the air—to be plucked to safety by Lucky, ready and waiting on the branches below.

A deep, primeval rage engulfed the Cloudfoot. He smashed into the Major with all his might. Nimlet wasn't thinking; he had only one aim—he went for the kill.

Nimlet was lost in a red haze of rage, blood pounding in his ears. Then one voice reached him: clear, and strong, and *right*. It was Lucky.

"Nim, stop—please stop!" cried his friend. "You're not a killer! It's not the Cloudfoot way!"

In shame, Nimlet released his hold, and the Major staggered backward, reeling with pain. In a blind panic, paws scrabbling frantically on the branch, he slipped. Nimlet lunged to grab his paw—but too late. The Major went tumbling from the tree.

On the ground, far below, a West Highland terrier had just trotted out for his morning walk. He was snuffling around the undergrowth, happily following scent trails, but at the sound of a screaming squirrel he froze.

His ears pricked up and his muscles tensed. The small white dog looked up to the trees just in time to see the animal falling directly toward him.

This time Finlay was too late.

"Gotcha!" said Jock, grinning.

30

The Word of Ma

The Fleet army had withdrawn and the Albion trees were safe once again. Two exhausted dogs and one small fox cub trotted up Park Road. Amber was going to be in deep trouble with her mother when she got back to the home-den. But who cared? Being a police fox was fun!

"So, what we going to do tomorrow?" she asked.

"*We* aren't doing anything tomorrow," growled Finlay.

"Go on, Fin," said Eric. "She could come on patrol with us, couldn't she?"

"Patrol?" said Finlay, horrified. "Foxes can't patrol. They can't follow orders!"

"I can follow orders—honest!"

"Yeah, go on, Fin, give her a chance. She was great at the Albion." Eric and Amber looked at him imploringly.

Blood and bone, thought the police dog, *I know I'm going to regret this.*

The Ma requested a meeting with the Honorable Mistress Tarragon Fleet. Lucky, Nimlet, and Mazie escorted her through the trees.

"Ooh-ooh, I suppose I'm going to have to go home today—I've got to go back to look after my Family. There's a lot to do."

"Of course, Honorable Mistress," said Lucky formally.

"Ooh-ooh, don't be silly. We're all friends. You don't have to call me that!"

"But you're Head of the Family Fleet now," said Nimlet. "That's—that's like being the Ma!"

"And *you* have saved my *life*—so you will *all* come to visit the Northend, whenever you like."

Nimlet looked doubtful. "We might not be allowed."

"Nonsense," said Tarragon haughtily. "I'm in charge now and I shall command it!"

She's going to be very good at giving orders, thought Lucky.

They reached the Meeting Drey, and a very official-looking Daughter Attendant ushered Tarragon inside.

It was plain that this meeting was private. For the first time in the history of the Avenue, Cloudfoot and Northender sat down to talk. The Ma was very impressed with the young female. She may not have learned the Knowledge, but she was eager to understand Cloudfoot ways and share them with her Family.

"There will be no more raids from the Family Fleet, Great Ma; we shall be your allies. But I cannot speak for the rest of the Families," Tarragon declared.

"Yes, they are a feral bunch," said the Ma sourly.

"No more feral than you would be, ma'am, if there was no space in your trees and your young were always hungry," said Tarragon, suddenly sharp and serious.

The Ma stiffened her whiskers; this female was full of surprises—what a pity she wasn't a Cloudfoot! "I see. So what do you suggest?"

"Ooh-ooh," said Tarragon brightly, "I've got *lots* of ideas . . ."

The Ma was very pleased. It would be a long and difficult branch to travel, but Tarragon's ideas might just work. Yes, why not trade with the Northenders, each clan learning from the other? *We could all be allies . . . it would take time . . . a united Avenue . . .* Another thought struck her: *They will call me "Great Ma the Peacemaker"!* Yes, the idea was very pleasing.

She did not, however, seem pleased when Lucky, Nimlet, and Mazie were summoned into the Meeting Drey. "We are hard pushed to know where to begin," she said coldly. "It seems that none of you can obey orders, and one of you is a defector to the camp of our *former* enemy." She fixed them all with her beady eyes. "Would any of you like to honor us with an explanation?"

Mazie stepped forward and bobbed formally. "Ma'am, as senior female of the group I take all responsibility."

"I'm sure you do, Miss Trimble," said the Ma coldly, "and I expect First Daughter will be having stern words with you later—but I would like to know what these *gentlemen* have to say for themselves."

Oh no! thought Nimlet, his whiskers trembling violently. *We are so in for it!* He gave Lucky an imploring look.

He could fight a horde of Northenders, thought Lucky, *but when it comes to facing the Ma he's petrified.*

"Thanks, Nim!" he mouthed, and stepped boldly forward. "Ma'am, I would like to say that the plan was ours, but the idea was Mistress Tarragon's."

"So you are blaming the Head of the Family Fleet for your actions?" said the Ma icily.

"No, ma'am!" said Lucky, horrified. "I'm giving her the *credit*! Northenders have to win honorably. Mistress Tarragon was sure they'd retreat if they were told the truth about her uncle's plot. Nimlet pretended to defect so that he'd be close by to protect her—so that she'd be heard."

This was not what the Ma had expected. "Indeed?" she said, impressed despite herself. "And did Mistress Tarragon advise you to leave your home-tree when First Daughter had expressly told you to stay?"

Lucky's tail twitched uncomfortably. *Here it comes*, he thought. *The inevitable judgment.* He'd failed the Run, disobeyed orders, and obviously wasn't "Cloudfoot material."

"No, ma'am," he admitted miserably. "I just wanted to rescue my friends and protect the Avenue."

"I see," said the Ma; she seemed deep in thought.

"Pardon my interruption, Great Ma," said Tarragon, "but if you intend to Cast Down these males, I will offer them a place in the Family Fleet trees. They are my friends and I am in their debt."

"A generous offer, Mistress Tarragon, but I fear that will not be possible."

Lucky and Nimlet didn't dare look at Tarragon or Mazie. This was awful.

The Ma stood up stiffly and looked the two squirrels over. "Gentlemen, our Avenue has always had need of brave and dedicated Defenders," she declared. "Squirrels who are Cloudfoot material, through and through." There was a pause . . . then her old face broke into a smile. "If *ever* there were two squirrels worthy of the name Cloudfoot, it is Mr. Lucky and Mr. Nimlet!"

Mazie gasped in surprise, and Tarragon clapped her paws in delight. Lucky and Nimlet just stared in openmouthed amazement.

Had the Ma *really* just said that?

"Gentlemen, you will both be joining the Watch and Patrol—and that," she said firmly, "is the Word of Ma!"

Red vs. Gray

"It doesn't matter how many times you see a squirrel, it's always exciting!" That's what my daughter used to say—and she's so right.

Squirrels live happily in our city parks and take full advantage of any human food that might come their way—but they're not tame, they're not pets. Squirrels are the closest thing many of us get to a wild animal, and watching them is fascinating.

The red squirrel in my story is a dainty creature with a bristly thin tail and spiky ear tufts. The gray squirrel is heavier and stockier, with round ears and a fuller tail. Which squirrel you usually see will depend very much upon where in the world you live.

The native squirrels in North America are generally gray. It's the red squirrel that's native to the United Kingdom and mainland Europe—but in 1876 a pair of North American grays were brought over to England and released in a park. People liked the look of the "new" squirrels—they were a novelty—and grays were shipped in all over the country, even to Regent's Park in London. It was a disaster for the native reds.

A lot of people believe that the grays were aggressive invaders. They weren't. They were just doing what any wild animal does—surviving and reproducing. The problem was that gray squirrels were better at it than the reds. They could eat a wider variety of foods, travel farther distances, and, most importantly, they were immune to squirrel pox virus and other diseases that could kill the reds. Worse, they could carry the virus unharmed and spread it among the red community. By the time people realized what was happening and made the red squirrels a protected species, it was too late. The grays had moved into most of the red squirrel habitats in the United Kingdom.

Some colonies of reds survive in Scotland and northern parts of England, others on islands where the grays have never been introduced. The reds in mainland Europe are similarly protected and are still thriving as the native species—but keeping the grays out is a continuous battle.

If you want to know more about red squirrel conservation, try these websites:

UK RED SQUIRREL GROUP
www.forestry.gov.uk/fr/ukrsg

RED SQUIRREL SURVIVAL TRUST
www.rsst.org.uk

SAVE OUR SQUIRRELS
www.saveoursquirrels.org.uk

Chris Hill

Acknowledgments

To the Honorable Mistress Beverley of the Family Birch, my wonderful editor and mentor—thank you.

To Rosemary Stones, who read my first faltering chapters and gave me the confidence to continue. Dogged appreciation goes to Harry Hound, Millie Mutt, and their humans, especially Corporal B. for the military input. Thanks to Detectives B. & T. for the policing information, and also to my youngest critics, Alvise and Molly, and my sternest, Andrew.

For the support, help, love, and general putting-up-with-me, I thank my own clan, Richard, Sam, and Alice.

Finally . . . *Lucky* would not have been possible without Barry Cunningham, who championed and nurtured the idea through all its manifestations. Thank you for believing in the squirrels.